THE JIGSAW PUZZLE

Cheryl Russell

Other Books by Cheryl Russell

Lily of the Valley
The Necklace
Evening Treats A collection of short stories
The One Who Got Away
Gallows Lane
A Bruised Reed
Murderous Feet
Missing
A Place of Safety

PROLOGUE

"Arbeit Macht Frei."

This was the sign above the gates of the camp Jacob and Sarah had just arrived at along with hundreds of others. They were pulled out of the cattle trucks and many stumbled and fell only to be hit with guns from the guards forcing them to hurry up.

Jacob and Sarah looked at each other, fear in their eyes. What would happen to them now? This was no good place, that they knew. They could see people in the distance inside the camp wearing some kind of uniform and looking like walking skeletons. They held hands as they moved forward in the group of people. Some tried to run away but were soon shot by the guards who were warning everyone to keep moving.

The couple were desperate for food and water as very little had been given them on the long journey cramped up in the trucks. It was standing room only and many had perished on the way, the weaker ones and the elderly. Jacob and Sarah were a strong, young couple. They had only been married a year and were still very much in love.

Jacob had been a lawyer in his previous life and Sarah a teacher. They had both lived in Munich. They had lost their jobs long ago and were kept hidden by friends who were sympathetic to their plight and against the Nazi regime. They never stayed in one place long, always moving around so as not to be caught if anyone should betray them. They didn't want their friends to be in trouble and probably shot for daring to help Jews. Jews were the enemy of the Nazi regime, people not thought fit to associate with the so called purity of the Aryan race.

They had lived like this for a few years, moving from one friend to another under cover of darkness and during the curfew. They had wanted children but were so grateful to God that it hadn't happened yet. They didn't want to bring children up in such a world where they were forced into hiding just to stay alive.

Sarah often had nightmares and had to be soothed by Jacob. Sometimes he had to put his hand over her mouth to stop her screams from being heard by neighbours or anyone outside making sure the curfew was being enforced.

During the day they had to stay very quiet, not making any sound. Conversations were conducted in whispers.

Their luck ran out in 1941 when someone had seen them enter a property during the night and had informed on them the next day. It was pure malice that had made the informer take action having a dispute with the occupiers of the property and saw this as a good way of getting their revenge.

Jacob and Sarah were quickly put on the cattle trucks and taken to Auschwitz in Poland on discovery that they were Jews although didn't practice their faith. That didn't matter to the Germans, all they cared about were their religion at birth. The family hiding them were shot.

It soon became apparent to Jacob that they were going to be split up. Further down the line he noticed that male and females were forced into two different lines going in different directions. He clung on to his love as long as he could until Sarah was roughly grabbed and pulled away from his clasp. Something inside told him he would never see his darling wife again. He pushed the thought away. That was of no help at all. He needed to keep hoping that one day this madness would end and they would be reunited and free to live their lives openly. Little was he to know how difficult life was going to be in the camp and how hope was so easily stripped away as life got harder and harder for the unfortunate inmates of Auschwitz Birkenau.

CHAPTER ONE

June 1946

Jacob stared straight ahead, not blinking, not speaking, not moving. The nurses looked at him with compassion but not knowing how to help him. He had been in that hospital bed since January when he was discovered on the road side barely alive. They had tried to nurse him back to health but he was still painfully thin. He had to be fed as he was in a world of his own and took no notice when they handed him the utensils to feed himself. He was lost to the world. The nurses often discussed him amongst themselves and marvelled that he had survived at all. Not only surviving what was now known as a death camp but also still alive all these months later which no one had expected. They couldn't even begin to imagine what traumas he had gone through and what he must have witnessed. They just continued looking after him wondering if this was going to be as good as he got. They hoped not as at some point if this state of affairs continued he would end up being transferred to an institution. Staff, doctors and nurses were trying to avoid that and hoping they would get through to him at some point. They didn't even have a name for him.

Jacob heard what was being said when he was spoken to but he had no ability to respond in anyway. The words always seemed to come from a long way off. He lay very still, not moving as if paralysed. The hospital were sure he wasn't but couldn't know for certain while he lay in that catatonic state.

They often had people arriving at the hospital looking for lost relatives. They would view Jacob but a shake of their head revealed he was not belonging to them. Had he any family? Anyone who could have survived intact from the camps. It must be difficult trying to find relatives when so many were missing. It was utter chaos outside. The red cross were doing their best but there wasn't enough to help the influx of displaced persons mostly from all the camps and in bad condition themselves. Those who had survived in hiding were coming out of the woodwork and trying to find family. It wasn't just Jacob who was unknown taking up hospital beds. But Jacob was certainly a severe case. Many who were viewed were unrecognisable being only skin and bones. They needed nourishment but even then it was difficult. They looked older than their years, not surprising after all they had been through and the starvation added on top. Their treatment was inhumane and news was only just seeping out. It wasn't just one camp but many others as well. Hospital staff were constantly amazed at the resilience of human life, their ability to survive such conditions. What kept them going when all hope was lost and they lived with the constant threat of death.

Gas chambers had been discovered and ordinary men and women were horrified at what had been happening in their name. Mass murder on such a large scale was unheard of and the only crime being committed was to be born a Jew.

There was always a nurse sitting beside Jacob should he start to rouse out of his stupor and be disorientated and afraid. They spoke to him in a low voice and with kindness in hope that he would come round. It hadn't happened yet but they wouldn't give up on him. They spoke to him in German but had no idea what his nationality was and what language he spoke. It could be anywhere in Europe in fact from any of the Nazi occupied countries.

In some part of him Jacob was aware that he was no longer in that awful camp. For one thing he was laying on a comfortable bed not that hard wooden thing in the camp. Also he recognised the kindness of the voices that spoke to him. Such kindness he hadn't heard for a very long time, not since the arrest of him and his wife. Sarah? His beloved, what had happened to her? Was she in hospital somewhere wondering about him? Had she even survived? He knew from experience that many perished in the camp. He wished he had as well. It would have been better than being left to die on the side of the road when they were taken on a long walk out of the camp. When he had collapsed he had lain completely still not wanting to draw attention to himself. He was poked and prodded with a gun before being left alone. He remained like that, his survival instinct had kicked in even if he would have preferred to die. He would have been shot if they thought him still alive. He had been rescued by men speaking a foreign language and taken to a hospital. Not speaking the language he had no idea who they were.

He had eventually found himself in a hospital where German was spoken. He was surprised by the kindness shown to him, not realising the war was really over and he was free. Jews were now acceptable. The Fuhrer, Hitler was dead and the Nazi Party disbanded and it's members in hiding. He was unaware of any of this. Not being with it enough to take notice of what was said to him.

There was part of him that longed for his wife but also realised it was highly possible she had not survived. He had no idea how he would live without her. He didn't have a clue how to look after himself after so long in captivity. He was afraid of the world and probably would never get over what had happened to him. He only had to look at his arm as a constant reminder of all that he had been through. His prison number tattooed there for all to see for the rest of his life. A marked man.

On one particular day yet another lady arrived at the hospital looking for her family. Like all the others she was taken around the wards where unidentified patients were waiting. Maybe it would be their lucky day and they would see a relative who had survived.

The lady stopped at Jacob's bed. She looked for longer than necessary causing the nurse to hold her breath. Could they really have an identity for this man at last? The lady turned to the nurse, eyes shining with unshed tears and said in a shaky voice, "It's him. My husband. My Jacob come back to me."

The nurse did a dance in her head, so pleased they had an identity and a relative to claim this man. At least it would no longer be an institution. He would be released to the care of his wife when strong enough. It was to be hoped his recovery would speed up due to a close relative being on hand. They found this usually helped in other survivors of the horrors.

Jacob heard the voices but couldn't understand what was being said or who they belonged to. It could be anyone talking. He couldn't even know if they were talking about him, although part of him was sure they were. This lady was standing at the end of his bed looking down at him. There was something about her that sent shivers through him, even though she was smiling as she looked at him and there were tears in her eyes. There was a vague familiar aura about her which he could feel but how he knew her he didn't know. He wasn't sure he wanted to either. He continued to stare blankly ahead, wishing he could put his finger on where he knew her from. It was important somehow and at odds to what she was saying to the smiling nurse.

Sarah, his wife, he remembered now. But had she survived or not. He longed to be free of this hospital bed so he could search and find out what happened to her after they got separated. He wasn't even sure he remembered what she looked like it had been so long. He knew he had changed as well. He imagined she would look something like him, hollow faced, bones highly visible throughout his body, eyes sunken in their sockets. It was the look of so many other inmates of the now notorious camp.

CHAPTER TWO

Jacob opened his eyes and found himself moving his head around, his eyes flickering over his surroundings. The nurse sensing the movement spoke quietly to him, "Hello there, are you back with us? We've been worried about you. Your wife has been in everyday to see you for the past two weeks."

His wife? Surely not. He didn't remember seeing her, but then he didn't remember anything since leaving those gates behind.

"Where am I?" he croaked in a voice which hadn't been used in months.

"You're in hospital. It's over. I can't imagine what you must have been through, but it's finished now. You won't go through that again." Seeing a look of confusion on his face she continued, "It's over. The war finished. The Fuhrer is dead and Nazism gone with him. You are free to go about your life as you want to once you are well enough to leave here."

Jacob continued to feel disorientated and unsure.

"Don't worry. Everything will be ok and I'm sure your wife will be in this afternoon to see you so that will help. She has been here everyday for the past month since she came looking for you."

"My wife?"

"Yes, Sarah is her name. You are Jacob apparently."

"Sarah?"

"Yes, she said she was a teacher before and you were a lawyer until you both had it stripped from you and had to go into hiding."

Memories started coming back to Jacob as he listened to the nurse describe his previous life.

"The family hiding?"

"You mean the people hiding you?"

Jacob nodded, not wanting to speak more as it was hurting his dry parched throat.

"I don't know," said the nurse truthfully. She could imagine but didn't want to say anything to this patient who was still so very fragile. He was finally coming round and she didn't want to send him back into the catatonic state he had just emerged from.

The energy this conversation had taken was too much for Jacob and he resorted to staring into space again. The nurse seeing this continued to sit quietly. Heartened as she was by a brief response from him. Hopefully these lucid moments would continue and start to last longer each time. She couldn't wait to tell the others and of course his wife when she arrived.

Sarah was such an attentive wife who obviously loved her husband very much. The nurse just wondered if he would be the same person she remembered because of all he had been through which they couldn't even begin to imagine.

As usual that afternoon during visiting hours Sarah made the long walk down the ward, passed all the other men in their beds and some sitting out.

Jacob was as usual lying on his back with his eyes staring vacantly. The nurse stood up with a look of excitement on her face as she turned to look at Sarah.

"He turned his head and we spoke earlier," she said before Sarah had a chance to say anything.

Sarah's face lit up but there was just something about the eyes that didn't quite match the look on her face, thought the nurse but shrugged it off quickly as her imagination. Sarah was the most attentive, devoted wife she had come across. It was probably due to them being parted for so long.

"Hello my darling, sweetheart," said Sarah, going to the side of the bed and kissing her husband's cheek.

Jacob didn't move or speak. Sarah looked at the nurse who shrugged.

Inside Jacob was wrestling with himself, he didn't know what was going on. He darted a look of confusion at the nurse who saw it and wondered. He didn't think he knew this woman coming to kiss him. It didn't look like anyone he knew, but then he couldn't remember much about his past. His memories were more recent of the time in the camp and being left for dead on the side of the road. He remembered nothing since then or prior to then either.

"This is your wife, Sarah," said the nurse.

Jacob said nothing but somehow the nurse knew he wouldn't, not in Sarah's hearing anyway. Feeling that Sarah's presence might be making things worse for him she suggested that Sarah leave.

"I can't leave him, I've only just arrived. I want him to recognise me and get to know me again, we were so much in love you know. We lost everything." said Sarah.

This sounded sensible to the nurse but she had to do what she felt was in Jacob's best interests which at that moment was resting and not having visitors who he couldn't seem to remember.

She urged Sarah away and told her to come back the next day and hopefully Jacob would be more responsive by then. The nurse couldn't be sure but she thought she saw a look of relief cross Jacob's face which puzzled her but remembering he didn't appear to recognise his wife so it was understandable really. The memories were bound to start coming back in time, as long as this wasn't rushed in any way. No pressure could be put on Jacob.

When the nurse returned after seeing Sarah out Jacob turned his head towards her and whispered a barely audible "Thank you."

"It's ok," said the nurse, trying to reassure him but not sure why it was needed.

Jacob closed his eyes and dozed off.

The shouting was getting louder, they were coming closer he could sense it. A guard broke into the hut and shouted at them all to get out. They dragged themselves out, except for those who were too sick or who had died. There were always some. In fact it was surprising it wasn't more considering how emaciated they all were.

Those who collapsed were sent to one side. The men tried to stay standing by all means knowing what would happen to them if they collapsed. They knew they would be sent to the "showers" and would never come out.

After role call they were put to work. Jacob sighed with resignation as he saw the guard who seemed to have it in for him personally. He knew it couldn't be true but that's how it felt. He would be whipped for no reason and shouted at. Maybe it was because he was German and understood the language whereas many had come from all over Nazi occupied Europe.

She came up to him face all screwed up in an awful sneer which he knew meant trouble. "I'll get you this time," she lifted the whip.

Jacob screamed.

"It's all right, you're safe. You're in hospital do you remember?"

Jacob nodded and turned to the nurse sat beside him.

"Hello there, it was just another nightmare. You're safe now."

Something inside Jacob told him he wasn't safe, but he had no idea why. He understood it was over and he would be ok but that niggle at the back of his mind told him otherwise. He knew the camps had been liberated and he was in hospital getting stronger.

"Sarah, your wife will be in later," said the nurse.

That was it! Sarah, it was something about her he was sure. He wished he knew what it was, but he just couldn't think. He shook his head.

The nurse seeing it said, "It's all right she understands. Just take your time. You'll get your marriage back on track you'll see. You will soon remember how happy you were and that can be rekindled now."

Jacob shook his head wishing he knew what it was that made him so uneasy then he would be safe, until then…….

CHAPTER THREE

"Come on love, why don't we go out for a walk in the grounds. Some fresh air will do you good," said Sarah, a week later when she visited.

Jacob shook his head. He didn't want to be alone with Sarah although she kept pushing it.

"I'll come with you," said the nurse.

Jacob would benefit from a little fresh air so she was happy to go with him if that made him more comfortable. He remained largely unresponsive to Sarah although was now able to chatter away to the nurses. They didn't understand what the problem was. Sarah was so loving and patient with him when she visited but he always held back. They had tried asking him what the problem was but he shrugged unable to remember the crucial fact he knew he needed.

Outside Jacob took a deep breath in wanting to savour the fresh air that he enjoyed feeling on his face. This was the first time he had ventured outside since he was found. Physically he was going from strength to strength and soon would be ready to leave the confines of the hospital.

They were concerned about his mental state though. The nightmares continued night after night and usually multiple times. This and his refusal to accept Sarah was worrying the hospital staff responsible for his wellbeing. They couldn't begin to imagine what he must have been through and were sure it was horrific as they learned more of the horrors inflicted on the Jews from those who had been involved in liberating the camps. News had filtered down throughout the country. So many of those involved had disappeared to avoid arrest and trial for war crimes against humanity. Some had been captured but others had not.

What was particularly worrying about the nightmares was that they had only started since Sarah had been on the scene. They couldn't understand it.

Jacob continued talking to the nurse as they walked around the grounds and ignored Sarah. She was a bit put out but she could wait. She didn't care how long. It would happen as she had planned. She had chosen him. She continued to love her husband in front of the staff, knowing Jacob would soon be sent home to continue to recuperate. She had found a lovely flat near the hospital that they would live in when he was released. They didn't have much stuff but that wouldn't bother them. They would buy as and when they could. For her purposes they wouldn't need much. As long as no one suspected everything would be find and she'd be safe.

Sarah had her own horrors and knew she would never go back to teaching again. She wasn't even sure she knew how to teach anymore, but she hoped Jacob would have something in mind.

Sitting on a bench they sat in silence, no one saying a word. Jacob too exhausted. He'd had enough for his first day outdoors and was ready to retreat back to the comparative safety of his bed. Deep down he knew they wouldn't keep him much longer now he could get out. They would discharge him into the care of Sarah and that he dreaded. It wouldn't matter to them that he didn't recognise her and was having dreadful nightmares about her. That was just part of the psychological effects of the trauma he had been through. The doctor had only told him that the previous day on his rounds. Jacob's weight was now much healthier and he looked a lot better. The hollows on his face had gone and the other bones were less obvious which was what the doctors were most concerned about. He was now responsive to staff at all times. It was now very rare for him to become catatonic although still happened occasionally. They had no idea where he went to when like that as he couldn't describe it to them. They didn't know if it was a good place or not but assumed it wasn't.

Sarah had reassured staff that she would be able to cope with him at home now. In fact she was desperate to have her husband to herself again for them to get to know each other in a way they couldn't at the hospital.

Doctors were talking about him going home in another week, during which time he would be encouraged to go outside more and more often in preparation of that.

Jacob had been told of the plans but this only served to make him more fearful but unsure why. Sarah had been very loving towards him he realised that, it was just he couldn't return it and he couldn't remember why. She was his wife, or so they'd said, but it didn't reassure him in any way. He felt very anxious when around her but again couldn't explain why. He had wondered if there were problems in the marriage prior to being taken and separated by the SS. He wished he could know. It might help explain to staff why he was so apprehensive, though whether they would believe him he was unsure. They were so taken in by Sarah's apparent love for him which they saw as genuine. He couldn't fault it either, but something still niggled at the back of his mind. He just couldn't grasp it and put it into words.

CHAPTER FOUR

The day had come. Jacob's tummy was churning with anxiety. The staff had told him this was normal having been in hospital so long and with the camp before. He had to get used to living in a free world again, where he could be whatever religion he wanted to and still be accepted for it. This wasn't helpful as he would still be living with Sarah who apparently couldn't wait to get him home again. There was still something not quite right in his mind although he was unsure what. It wasn't just that her smile didn't quite reach her eyes or that they were icy cold. She couldn't help the colour of her eyes he supposed. It was something else that didn't ring true somehow. There was nothing he could do about it as yet until he knew more. Getting home and getting to know her might help him reach the truth which he was sure was there somewhere. She wouldn't be able to keep up the façade much longer he was sure, no one could.

There was part of him hoping he was wrong and that she really was his wife and that they were as in love as she proclaimed they were.

He looked up and saw Sarah smiling as she walked down the ward to his bed. It didn't matter to her that she had wolf whistles as she went passed the other patients. She had only eyes for Jacob and that was the way she meant it to stay. As she approached she held out her arms for him to go into. He did as was expected, realising it would be wrong to let her know he was on to her especially as he had no idea what it was that wasn't quite right about her.

The nurses watched with smiles on their faces. They were so pleased his story had a happy ending, so many didn't these days. Too many people lost and alone. Families torn apart. The scale of Nazism was still coming to light. They had become fond of him over the last few months. They couldn't say what it was just something about him. Maybe because he had been so clearly traumatised and yet had come out the other side whereas so many didn't, forever locked into the horrors they had faced.

Jacob drew away from Sarah and looked her up and down. Yes, something was there. She had felt so stiff and wooden as she held him in the hug. He wished that was enough to arouse suspicions but it wouldn't be. It would be seen as an awkwardness after being apart for so long. He felt safe while he was in hospital but that was about to end. He had to move on to the next stage of his life.

"Are you ready darling?" asked Sarah, who was avoiding Jacob's eyes.

Jacob just nodded, sure if he spoke he would burst into tears and he didn't want to see the look of impatience on her face however fleeting it might be.

His favourite nurse came over to say goodbye. He embraced her and thanked all the nurses for all they had done for him.

He wasn't leaving completely ok as he still had frequent nightmares, but he was told that was to be expected. Sarah had said she felt confident to deal with anything which might arise. She was just desperate to get him home again so they could start living a normal life, whatever that was.

Sarah leading the way they left the hospital and went out into the bright sunlight. Jacob shielded his eyes against it. He was still unused to the light as it had always been dull days in the camp, or that was how it seemed.

He held on to Sarah's arm as they walked along the road. He was feeling very disorientated and frightened as they continued. He wished they could have visited their flat before being discharged so it wasn't too strange for him. He understood this wasn't where they had lived originally but Sarah had found what she could and they would have to make the best of it. There were so many displaced people wandering around aimlessly. Unsure what to do or how to live again.

He walked on the inside of Sarah, not wanting to be near the road where army trucks drove by every few minutes or so it seemed. The thought had even occurred to him that maybe Sarah would even try and push him into it in front of a vehicle. He didn't know why he should think like this as she had never actually harmed him or threatened him in anyway.

"Down here," said Sarah pointing down a narrow alley way. "I know it seems grotty but this was the best I could do under the circumstances. We're lucky, so many still have nowhere to live."

Jacob tried not to wrinkle his nose at the stench which hit him as they turned down the alley. He wasn't sure what it was, rotten cabbage maybe? He suddenly gave a shriek as he saw a rat run across his shoe.

"Yes I know, sorry about that. They are everywhere at the moment. You'll get used to them eventually. I did and now I don't notice them anymore."

"We had fleas at the camp," said Jacob speaking for the first time since leaving the hospital.

"That's over and done with now darling. Let's not think about it." Sarah gave a shudder at the thought of something so distasteful.

"But it was a big part of our lives we can't just pretend it never happened. We won't get over it so quickly," said Jacob.

"We have to move on or we'll never be happy again."

"What do you mean? I can't pretend it never happened," said Jacob repeating himself, but not knowing what else to say in response.

Sarah withdrew his arm and turned to face him. A look crossed her face which he couldn't describe but it gave him goose bumps up and down his spine. Why could no one see what she was really like and find out who she really was. All he knew was she wasn't his Sarah. Even one changed drastically it wasn't her. He felt in danger from this one and the Sarah he only had vague memories of would never hurt anyone and he was sure she wouldn't have changed personality so completely whatever she had had to endure.

"Come on, up the steps," Sarah said rather impatiently.

Jacob tried to quicken his pace but couldn't, still a bit weak from his ordeal.

Following her he stepped through the front door. He looked around, she had got the place looking nice he had to give her that. Sarah gave a small smile seeing his approval. It was certainly better than the outside.

Two upright chairs stood in front of a fire place where they could sit and warm themselves in the winter months. The other end of the room sat a small table and a couple of chairs. A door the other side of the table revealed a kitchen. Not big, but enough to meet their needs. Along a small corridor there was a bathroom and a bedroom, again very small but adequate.

Jacob being tired sat on the double bed and then lay down, ready for a long rest. He was not used to being out of bed for so long.

"Come on," said Sarah, "There is no time for sleeping. It's lunch time and I thought we could have some salad at the table properly."

"Can't you bring it in here. I really need the rest."

"Darling I'm not your slave, I'm not bringing food here for you. You can come and get it for yourself and sit down and make conversation. We have a lot of time to make up for."

He recoiled as he heard the hardness in her voice that couldn't be disguised even if she tried, which she didn't.

Slowly standing up Jacob sighed, "I'm so tired from just getting here. I need a rest regularly at the moment."

"As I said just now I'm not your slave so get up and stop being so lazy."

Jacob was uncertain how to react to this. Although he had been suspicious about her true identity there had been nothing obvious until now. If only the hospital had seen this side of her. There was a threatening note to her voice which Jacob felt intimidated and frightened by. It was like being back in the camp again. Auschwitz Birkenau, he now knew it to be called. He'd heard there were others spread around which housed and killed large numbers of Jews.

"Which camp were you in?" he asked.

"None of your business."

"It is if we are man and wife. I want to know what you went through. It's some common ground we have in which to build a new marriage on."

Sarah shrugged. "I don't like to talk about it."

Jacob didn't know how to respond. It was like trying to communicate with an alien. They seemed to have nothing in common and he didn't know how to get passed that.

He followed Sarah to the kitchen where he helped prepare some salad and they took it through to the table.

"Well," he said. "You wanted us to sit at the table to eat together so what do you want to talk about."

Sarah shrugged. "Nothing in particular. It's just I refuse to be your slave. In future this will be your job."

"But I'm the man I'm supposed to go out to work while you stay at home and cook meals for us to enjoy together."

"You haven't got a job, if that hasn't escaped your notice."

"But I'll have to start looking for work. We can't get back on our feet if neither of us do anything."

"Who says we aren't doing anything. I've got a job cleaning at a hotel. It's better than nothing. How do you think I managed to afford this place if I wasn't working. Get real."

Jacob said nothing. What was their to say in response to that? He didn't know how to meet Sarah halfway. This was not working out and he wished he could go back to the hospital where he was cosseted and felt safe. Now they were home she was certainly making her true colours known. This wasn't the loving wife she had shown at the hospital, but another altogether side which he didn't like at all. He had a bad feeling that he would find it difficult to get away from her if he tried. He filed the thought away for another time if it should prove necessary to get away and get help. First he really needed to find out who she was and a bit about her background. He didn't know how to go about it but hopefully she would relax and reveal more if he didn't try and push it. She was very much on guard and wouldn't say anything whilst under pressure. No, he had to wait for things to slip out and then he would have something to go on if he needed to get the authorities involved. He realised he knew nothing about the way the country was now run. He had seen a lot of British army trucks around but that didn't mean anything as there were also American and Russian. He knew Hitler was no longer in power but didn't know what had happened. The nurses had always refused to talk about the unspeakable horror of the Nazi regime that was still coming out.

Sarah stood up and went to sit in one of the chairs.

"I'm going to bed now if you don't mind," said Jacob.

"Er who said you could. You didn't ask permission. You have to wash up and make me a cup of tea before you do anything."

Jacob carefully took the plates back to the kitchen and started the kettle boiling. His Sarah was quite a bully. Or should he use the term his Sarah as she didn't belong to him that was certain. She was her own woman.

Washed up and tea made, Jacob again attempted to go to bed.

"Why?" asked Sarah. "You can go later. It's too early if you go now."

Jacob sighed. There was nothing for it but to do as he was told, but he was so tired. He didn't know how to stay awake.

In the end Sarah had the solution. He started dozing, but every time it happened she prodded him with a stick she used for poking the fire. She was determined he would do as she commanded and if that meant using a stick then so be it she would do whatever it took. Under no circumstances were he to be head of the household. She was the boss and the sooner he learned that the better for both of them. Her true feelings must stay hidden until he was totally under her thumb where he belonged. He was a filthy Jew after all. She almost shuddered at the thought of having a relationship with one, but it was the only way she could stay safe. No one, not even Jacob was to be allowed to discover her true identity. The façade must continue.

"What was that for?" asked Jacob coming to after one prodding.

"You went to sleep."

"I'm tired. I still get tired easily and need to sleep."

"Not here you're not. It's pure laziness. You wouldn't have got away with that in the camps. You sleep when I say you can."

Jacob felt a flicker of fear. This wasn't Sarah. He couldn't imagine having married such a bully. Who was she? He wished he could remember the memories at the back of his mind. He needed help but how could he get it? Would he be left alone when he had to go back to the hospital for a check up? He could voice his concerns then. That's if they believed him as she kept up a good loving wife around others. The reality was completely different when alone.

Later when Sarah deemed it acceptable she suggested they went to bed.

"This is your room," she said, pointing out a tiny room with just a single bed in it. What she didn't reveal were the handcuffs she had managed to get hold of for when it proved necessary. She didn't need them yet, but at a later date she would use them. She tried to keep the smile from her face at this thought. It would give her great pleasure. For now things would be kept simple.

"Am I not sleeping with you darling?" asked Jacob.

"Not today. You only said earlier how tired you get and I want you to have a good nights sleep." This was said grimly. She couldn't bear the thought of having to be in the same bed and touch each other as married couples did.

Jacob went in and lay on the bed closing his eyes straight away. Sarah watched him dispassionately before leaving the room and turning the key in the door. She couldn't risk him trying to escape. Although she didn't think he would so soon she had to make certain.

Jacob opened his eyes, having heard the door shut. He thought he heard a key turning in the lock so he got up quietly and went to the door. Sure enough it was locked. What was he to do, something was very wrong here. Not for the first time he wondered who this woman was. He knew with certainty it wasn't his Sarah, if Sarah were really the name of his wife. He needed to find out more before he tried to get help. No one would listen at this point in time. Sarah was a good actress that was for sure.

Laying on the bed he tried to dredge some memory up. It didn't work and soon he felt his eyes get heavy and start to close. He tried to stay awake but his body's need for sleep betrayed him.

Sarah checked on him in the night but was satisfied nothing was needed he was fast asleep. She went back to bed and lay there. When would she get to see her Bruno? The real love of her life. They had plotted this between them and he was doing the same with another survivor of the camps. It was the only safe way of staying outside the radar of the authorities. They were going to do all they could to stay alive in these unsafe times. With the enemy ruling the country she couldn't take any chances.

CHAPTER FIVE

Jacob woke and rubbed his eyes. He looked around the room disorientated at first and wondering where he was. This didn't look like the hospital. Then he remembered he was home with his Sarah who might not be his much loved wife. He went to the door and this time found it open. He thought maybe he had imagined it being locked. Could it be part of a nightmare instead of the reality it had seemed to be last night. It could have been an hallucination he had been so tired. Outside the door he found a tray of food with a note.

Jacob,
I had to go to work. You were so fast asleep I didn't have the heart to wake you my darling. Enjoy your breakfast. I'll be back at lunchtime.
Sarah xxxxxxx

He went back to bed with a tray. He couldn't help but smile at the note it was something his loving Sarah would have done. Wait a minute, was that a memory coming back? He certainly hoped so. He just wished he didn't feel so confused.

He made short work of the tray, realising how hungry he really was. He hadn't felt like much yesterday being so anxious in a different environment. Maybe that was the reason Sarah didn't seem right. He must have imagined her antipathy towards him. Today would be the time to start again and try and build a loving relationship with her.

Very soon he found his eyes closing again and he dozed off.

He was running away from somewhere, but couldn't remember where from. He could hear footsteps getting closer and closer. He couldn't allow them to catch him or he would be shot. He was surprised that he hadn't heard any shots ring out.

"Wake up, wake up," said a voice, shaking him out of his nightmare.

He opened his eyes and looked straight at his Sarah. "Sorry I must have been having a bad dream again."

"It's all right," she said.

"Will I ever be free of it?"

"You will in time. You know what the hospital said. It would take time to get over all that you've been through."

He smiled. "At least I've got you. I can get through anything with you by my side."

He went to embrace Sarah but she pulled away with a look that could only be described as disgust. It worried him and reminded him that something wasn't right. He had convinced himself that she was who she said she was.

"Come on you should get up for lunch. We'll have it together then I must get back to work."

Jacob nodded and followed her to the dining room table where a nice meal was laid out. He looked at the food and almost gagged. He didn't feel up to eating.

"Can I have it later I'm not really hungry now?"

"You will sit down and eat with me. I'm not leaving food around for you to help yourself to. When you've recovered a bit more you will find yourself doing the cooking."

Jacob was surprised. In his world the women stayed at home and did the cooking for the men. It seemed the world was changing and he had better get used to it.

He picked up his knife and fork and began to eat slowly. He struggled to keep the food down with every mouthful. Something kept him trying. He couldn't be sure, but felt he would be punished if he were to be sick.

Sarah didn't look at him throughout the silent meal.

"Ok now we've finished you can wash up quickly before I have to get back to work."

"It's all right no rush. I'll do them when you've gone. I thought we should have a chat now. Try to get to know each other again."

"What is there to know? I'm Sarah your wife."

"I know that, but I can't remember much about you."

"You'll have to stay in suspense then as I want those things washed and for you to be back in your room again."

"Must I? If I go back to bed I'll sleep and then it will be even harder tonight. I could stay through here sitting in a chair."

"Oh no you don't. You do as I say. I'm the boss around here."

Jacob shrugged and stood up, reminded once again of the unease he felt around Sarah.

Washing up done, back in his room laying on the bed. Sarah had left for work and locked the door as she left. He had tried the handle and found it wouldn't move.

He tried not to panic. Something was very wrong and he needed help, but how was he to get help when he couldn't even leave the room. He went to the tiny window and attempted to open it only to find it was either stuck firmly or was locked. It wouldn't have surprised him to find it locked but he still tried giving Sarah the benefit of the doubt.

Sarah felt trapped in the situation with Jacob. She knew it was her fault as Bruno hadn't wanted them to do this but she had convinced him it was for the best. How she missed her lover. It had been the only way. If she was careful she wondered if it would be possible to meet up with her love.

Of course they would have to be very discreet and make sure they weren't being followed. She would write to him and suggest it she supposed. She gave a genuine smile at the thought. It could be fun, she just had to hope that Bruno agreed and was able to get away.

It was easier for him with his 'wife'. Men were more easily accepted as bullies and the female as submissive so it was nothing for him to cope with. In some ways she wished she hadn't thought of this idea as it was hard work and more difficult with Jacob than imagined. She didn't know what she would do if the rest of his memory came back. She would be in a difficult position. She was perfectly happy to give the ultimate punishment if necessary but it would leave her vulnerable again and that she wasn't prepared for.

CHAPTER SIX

Jacob spent his time waiting for Sarah to get home from work in deep thought. There was nothing else to do locked in a room. He wished he could reach into the dark recesses of his mind and retrieve the information he knew was there. It wouldn't free him from this situation but at least he might understand why he was in it. He was certain now that Sarah was not his wife but he also felt it was safer to go along with the subterfuge. He needed to work out who she really was and then try and find an escape route. Maybe he would get more clues from her as time went on.

Laying on the bed with hands behind his head he tried to relax. Maybe the truth would come if only he could let go of the tension inside that was building up as fear grew. He longed to get outside and breathe in some fresh air. He wasn't sure how fresh it was in that rundown area he was in but it had to be better than being stuck inside. It would also make him more aware of his surroundings when the time came to try and escape. No one knew of his existence so he wouldn't have any local friends who might help him. He was certain that Sarah wouldn't let him out on his own. Maybe she wouldn't even let him out with her. She probably wanted to keep him hidden.

Jacob felt himself drifting off. He tried shaking himself to wake up and think but couldn't manage it. The truth could come to him in his sleep he supposed so he stopped fighting it.

"Come on lazy bones it's time to wake up," said Sarah shouting in his ear as he wasn't responding any other way. She felt a bit frightened which she didn't like. She preferred to be in charge. She couldn't bear to lose him this soon into her plan. Further down the line maybe when his usefulness ran out, but who knew when that would be.

Jacob heard a voice calling to him from somewhere outside of himself but couldn't quite grasp hold of it, so deep was he in sleep. He didn't realise it was no ordinary sleep. If he had known he might have made some excuse not to eat and drink everything laid out for him.

Sarah shook him, thoroughly frightened now. Bruno had told her how much to give him to knock him out, but what if she had misheard and given him too much or if Bruno had deliberately told her wrong. All these thoughts went through her mind.

Going through to the kitchen she began to prepare a meal for them both. It hadn't been her plan to cook it should have been his job.

Meanwhile Jacob began to stir slightly. He opened his eyes, feeling very sluggish and drugged. He could hear noises which told him Sarah was home. He lay there with his eyes half open thinking. Could he get her to reveal more information. If he could he would have to be clever about it.

Footsteps moving towards the door. Jacob shut his eyes not wanting his so called wife to realise he was awake now. He felt it was important although he had no idea why. It might fill her with fear giving him some power back into this uneven relationship.

Sarah opened the door and shouted at him to wake up. She put the food down and went for the poker again. This should rouse him if nothing else did. She poked and prodded him but got no response. She looked closely at his face for any signs of a grimace but nothing. He seemed deep in unconsciousness. She wished she knew if he were alive but had no first aid training. Her training had been in punishing others and being cruel to the scum of the earth – the Jews.

What do I do now? she wondered. Scared as she was she didn't want to call for help and draw attention to herself. She wished she could contact Bruno but knew he couldn't come to the apartment. They couldn't be seen together, not yet, maybe not for a long time to come. Sarah sighed. Would she ever be really free? Maybe it was right to give herself up now and not stay in hiding. She was sure the hospital would confirm Jacob's state. They knew him and would just assume he had retreated back into catatonia again.

Jacob sensed Sarah standing there watching him. Oh what fear she must be feeling he thought. It would give her some idea of the feelings she was inflicting on him, although he could feel she had a lot more up her sleeve.

He slowly opened his eyes to face her. He could see the relief on her face when she realised she hadn't killed him, however close it might have been.

"Here's dinner. I won't be eating as I'm going out for the evening with an old friend." She couldn't admit it was her lover or it would give the game away. She couldn't do that at this early stage. She needed him to be dependent on her. It shouldn't be too difficult.

Jacob took the tray from her and thanked her politely. It would do no good to antagonise her so soon.

He ate slowly which irritated Sarah who wanted him to hurry up so she could get going and he would have more thoughts over her true identity. He knew without any doubt that he knew her in his past life but didn't know who she was or who she had become. The more he tried to remember the harder it became. Somehow he felt that he was better off not knowing but that wouldn't change his current circumstances.

"Hurry up, I haven't got all night," said Sarah holding the poker menacingly.

Jacob, realising he was annoying her continued to eat slowly. It was the only way he could feel some power and control over the situation. He didn't have much appetite which helped validate his controlled eating.

"This is no joke, you eat or I remove it. This is the last time you will get any food or drink today as I will not be back early."

"Can I come with you? It's time we went out and did something as a couple."

"Not today, I'm meeting an old friend and you would be bored. We'll just be chatting about old times."

Jacob nodded wondering who she was seeing. He wished he could follow her, that might lead him to the truth about her identity.

Jacob hurriedly finished his meal not wanting to trigger her wrath any further. He could see she was close to the edge because of him. He let Sarah lead him back to his room before she went out.

"What time will you be back?"

"None of your business."

"It is, you're my wife and I'll worry about you. It's dark out there."

"Don't worry about me I'm a survivor. You just rest this evening."

Jacob breathed a sigh of relief when Sarah left. It was good to be alone to think. Somewhere deep within wanted to confront her and find out who she really was. His Sarah had been a gentle person but this one was the complete opposite in personality and seemed to hate him. Yes, they had been through a lot which could be enough to change a person but his gut told him this wasn't his wife. If she wasn't then he needed to find out who she was and why she had decided to impersonate her. What had happened to the real Sarah? Had she even survived the horrors of Auschwitz? There were too many questions going round and round in his head. He had no idea how to go about getting the answers especially as he couldn't get out being kept under lock and key.

....

Sarah flung her arms around her beloved Bruno. It was so good to see him again. To see his eyes light up at the sight of her. She was no beauty she knew that but he only had eyes for her. To him she was a rare find, the snow white in the mirror.

"How's it going," he asked in his abrupt way.

"It's hard when I so much want to be with you openly."

"It was your idea," he said. "You know I didn't want to go along with it. I'd have much rather taken my chances. We might have been able to get out of the country and somewhere safe."

"This is my home. I didn't want to leave it. Germany has to be great again one day when we shall lead again."

Bruno shook his head. She really had buried her head in the sand. They would never be entirely safe he knew that. Nazism would not be back. As much as he had admired Hitler he also had a mind of his own and knew they had gone too far. Sarah was much more an ardent fan than himself.

"I'm not giving up. We have to win this is just a temporary blip you'll see."

"Come on let's find somewhere to eat, I'm starving." Bruno was desperate to change the subject. Given the chance she could go on and on about how wonderful Hitler was and what good work could be done until such a time as they took over again.

Sarah followed her lover into a nearby fine restaurant and bar. They placed their order then Sarah looked at her hands. She didn't like her hands being dirty or sticky in any way.

"You know, I don't think we needed to carry out your whole plan because with the number tattooed on our arms everyone will assume we were survivors of the horrors carried out."

"I don't want to take that risk. Don't worry I'm sure it won't be for long and then we can openly be together again as ourselves."

"Hilde, you know I don't agree, I've said so often enough. We won't get to power again. The enemy has taken over our country and isn't going to leave anytime soon."

"How many times do I have to tell you my name is Sarah. You have to be more careful. What if the wrong person is listening?"

"Sorry," sighed Bruno.

Bruno, not for the first time, wished he had never taken up with Sarah. She was much more extreme than he had ever been. He went along with the Party line because he had no choice but he had hated it. He hated how she expected him to treat his Jewish "wife". Not for the first time he was starting to feel sorry for Jacob and what he must be going through with Sarah as his wife. He knew he was kept under lock and key and was given drugs to make him sleep just to keep him quiet. If he wasn't so weak maybe he would tell the authorities what was happening. It might be the end for him but he wasn't sure he cared. He deserved everything he got for what he had been made to do. It was still an option but he was so much under Sarah's thumb he couldn't bring himself to do it and yes he was still in love with her. The problem was that he saw her flaws now. To begin with he couldn't see any wrong in her, she had been perfect in his eyes. Unfortunately he didn't think she would ever change. Totally brainwashed by Hitler and his cronies.

CHAPTER SEVEN

Jacob opened his eyes with a start. He was sure he had heard a noise. He sat up in bed and listened. Yes, there it was again. Someone was moving around. He wished he knew who it was. He didn't know if Sarah was back yet as he'd once again fallen asleep soon after she'd left him. He was worried by all this sleeping he was doing. He hadn't been sleeping this much when in hospital. He couldn't query it with a doctor as he was sure Sarah wouldn't let him see anyone about it.

He stood up, sitting back down straight away as dizziness over took him. What was wrong with him. He was weaker and more ill than in hospital. It didn't make sense.

Trying again, this time he managed to stay on his feet and crept to the door. He tried the door handle and once again found it locked. It disturbed him that she felt a need to lock him in one small room. He crept back to bed not wanting anyone to know he was there and awake. He lay back on the bed and closed his eyes. He kept them closed even when he heard a key turning in the lock and the door opening.

Sarah approached the bed quietly and looked down at her husband. Her lips were curled up in a sneer as she watched his sleeping form. Leaving the room she once again locked the door.

She wasn't going to take any chances although she was sure he didn't suspect anything untoward yet.

Jacob opened his eyes when he heard the door locking again. It had been so hard to stay still without actually tensing up. It wouldn't do for Sarah to see he was really awake. He was sure she would have some punishment up her sleeve and not just the poker.

While he was awake he went back to thinking. Try as he might he couldn't come up with any identity for her. He was sure he knew her though and that thought was getting stronger in his mind. He just couldn't get at the memory. It was so frustrating. He longed for his memory to return.

There was even part of Jacob that wondered if this was his Sarah. Maybe she hadn't been the person he thought she was, it could have been an act and now she was showing her true colours. Even as he thought it, it seemed silly to him. Nothing about it made sense. He was going mad, stuck in these small four walls with just a bed and handcuffs on the bed which hadn't been used yet but he was in no doubt they could be in the future. Things were not going to get better any time soon.

He turned over on his side and stifled a yawn. Time to go back to dreamland. He shut his eyes and let himself drift off.

………

"Wake up, wake up," said Sarah, shaking Jacob roughly.

"Wha…what is it?"

"You were screaming. You'll wake the neighbours if you keep on like that."

For a moment he thought she actually might care about him, but realised all she cared about was disturbing others. He suspected no one knew of his existence and were never going to find out.

"Sorry. It must have been another nightmare."

"Well try and keep quiet," the unsympathetic Sarah said.

"Sorry I didn't know I was making any sound I was asleep until you shook me awake."

"You'll have to sort yourself out."

"How can I. I went through hell that isn't just going to go out of my mind in minutes. It's impossible."

Sarah shrugged.

"I'm surprised you aren't the same. You must have gone through what I did, I've seen your number tattooed on your arm."

Sarah's hard features softened momentarily. "I know it's hard, but we have to let it go and forgive them for what they did to us."

"You really think it's that simple?" he asked, incredulity in his voice.

"I do."

"It's the only way to really heal."

"I'll give it a go and see what happens. If you can then I'm sure I can. What time is it by the way?"

"Four o clock. So settle down again and close your eyes."

"I'm scared to in case the same thing happens again."

"It's ok I'm right here beside you. You're safe nothing can harm you now."

Jacob closed his eyes as directed but didn't sleep. His thoughts were going round and round. He was confused. Sarah had been so harsh and insisting he not make a sound but then she seemed to melt and be understanding of what he was going through. He had to admit he didn't know if he were coming or going. How could she just change like that? Who was the real Sarah? The mean, bullying one or the gentle understanding one that he'd just caught a glimpse of.

…………..

Sarah sat beside Jacob while he slept exactly as she'd promised. She had nearly slipped up then. He had caught her out. Of course his real wife would have been nicer about it because she would have understood had she survived. She needed to be much more careful in future. It couldn't hurt her to be nice occasionally, it would keep him on his toes and make him question things in his mind. If she were nice he would be less likely to suspect anything, but how could she bring herself to change attitude towards a Jew.

She found her own eyes closing again so laid down beside Jacob on the bed. She lay as far away as possible and kept herself very tense. She found the whole experience cringe worthy. How could she lay with a Jew? Bruno would hate her for it she was sure of that. But he didn't need to know. It was between Jacob and herself.

Jacob opened his eyes as he felt her relax beside him. He wasn't asleep but had obviously convinced her that he was. He wondered if he could creep out while she was asleep and escape somehow. The problem was he was still very weak and wouldn't be able to move very fast so she was bound to catch up with him and he would end up worse than he was already.

Was Sarah a light sleeper he wondered. This would depend on how far he got. He didn't want to try anything too soon and fail as it would put her on top alert which wouldn't help his cause at all. Plus he still needed to have some idea of her real identity. Again he decided to play it safe for the moment and see what happened. Maybe she would relax around him if she thought he were behaving in the way she wanted him to.

Feeling thirsty he wondered if he could go and get a drink of water from the kitchen. He didn't see anything wrong in that but she might considering the door was kept locked. Sliding his feet to the floor he decided to risk it, after all what could be wrong with walking around their apartment. That was what normal people did and he wasn't in hiding now, or he shouldn't be anyway.

Creeping quietly he made it to the kitchen and had a lovely cold drink of water. It certainly went down well. He turned to make his way back to bed when he stopped abruptly. Sarah was standing in the doorway watching him. How long had she been there?

"What exactly do you think you're doing?"

"Just getting a drink of water. Sorry did I wake you. You looked so peaceful I didn't want to disturb you."

"What else were you going to do?" Sarah asked with a suspicious tone to her voice.

"Nothing," said Jacob. "I was just about to go back to bed." This was said very innocently to try not to arouse suspicion. It was also the truth but he wasn't sure that would make any difference to her.

Sarah nodded appearing to accept what he said. She wasn't sure she believed him but thought she needed to be careful. As long as she didn't make him suspect anything she would be safer. At this stage she wanted him to accept her for who she said she was.

"Ok darling, let's get you back to bed." Sarah almost spat the words out and choked over the word darling but was trying to force herself. Bruno had a point after all.

She followed closely on Jacob's heels as he went back to his room. He wasn't surprised when he got into bed that she left and locked the door behind her.

He realised he still hadn't earned her trust. He realised that was the next step he had to play her at her game and make her think he could be trusted to walk freely around the small space she called home.

The rest of the night passed uneventfully. Jacob dozed on and off but was too shaken by the nightmare earlier to really relax into deep sleep. His thoughts were also consumed with the mystery of who Sarah was. He was fairly certain she was no Jew although he could be wrong on that count. He didn't know enough about her and he had to find out more. At the same time he needed to be extremely careful because he was expected to believe she was his wife in which case he wouldn't need to ask loads of questions. There was only so far he could get away with playing the can't remember card.

CHAPTER EIGHT

"Why don't we sleep together darling?" Jacob asked innocently one day.

"You're still so unsettled I didn't want to rush you," Sarah responded after careful thought.

"I'm sure it would help me get better if we were cuddled up together."

Sarah tried not to cringe at this. Sleeping with a Jew was not something she could bring herself to contemplate. Not now, not ever. She didn't want to become infested by a load of Jewish parasites. Ugh, she shivered inside at the very thought.

"I'll think about it."

Jacob realised he wouldn't get any further on that subject. He had noticed the distaste that had crossed her face at his suggestion, although she had tried hard to disguise it. What did it mean? The Sarah he had known wouldn't have reacted like that, she had been very loving. Who knew what she had been through though. She wasn't talking about her suffering during those awful years.

Jacob was sat on the sofa getting very bored. Sarah no longer locked him in his room but he had no door key so couldn't go out. In fact the front and back doors were all locked so he was stuck in. Sarah quite often went out in the evenings and came back late, long after he had gone to bed. The reality was he hardly ever saw her, which for him was good. It gave him more thinking time. However, he couldn't do that forever as he was getting no further forward. He was starting to think he was going mad as he had started talking to himself.

....

Sarah was spending yet another evening with Bruno. They met up at least three times a week, deciding that they really couldn't keep away from each other. They talked about their respective partners and Bruno had persuaded Sarah she needed to let up on Jacob or he would start suspecting something was wrong.

Bruno had wanted Sarah to sleep with Jacob but that she couldn't do. It was a step too far in her eyes. She found it hard to ease off with the bad treatment of Jacob. He was only a Jew after all and deserved everything she could give out.

What Bruno wasn't saying was that he was starting to have feelings for the Jew he was living with. He was starting to see she wasn't the scum he had been led to believe, in fact she was just like anyone else with likes and dislikes and her own personality. As he got to know her he began to feel guilty with the part he played during the war.

He wished Sarah would come to this realisation as well, but everything he said went straight over her head. She was so hardened. If it wasn't for Sarah Bruno would probably have handed himself in. He deserved the severest punishment that could be meted out.

Sarah lay in his arms content and at ease, having no clue as to what was going on in his head.

"You know I think we should start spending the weekends together instead of just seeing each other evenings."

Bruno was startled at this statement. The original idea had been for them to keep away from each other until it was safe to be out in the open.

"What about our partners?" asked Bruno.

"What about them? They are nobody important. I feel starved of affection when I'm not with you."

Bruno sighed. "But we don't want them to get suspicious do we."

"They won't, I'll make sure of that."

"Oh no, I refuse to drug her up if that's what you're suggesting."

"Why not? It's the best way."

"No it isn't. We could make them very ill and that isn't part of the plan."

"So what, they are only Jews," Sarah said.

"They are human beings and are not expendable."

"Of course they're not. They're scum. You should be careful you don't know what you'll catch from them."

Sarah started to worry inwardly although she was careful not to let Bruno see it. He seemed to be moving away from her and to show concern for the Jew he lived with which was only supposed to be for convenience sake. She was losing her control which she hated. If necessary she would bring up the hold she had over Bruno, that would bring him back under control again.

"I won't catch anything she isn't ill and neither is your Jacob. He may not remember much before his time in Auschwitz but that's not contagious." Bruno looked seriously at Sarah and continued, "You know Sarah we were wrong to treat them as we did. Hitler brainwashed us but he had it wrong as well."

"You traitor how could you. The Fuhrer was absolutely correct. Just because he died doesn't mean we have to change our views. There are plenty who still share our values."

"He was weak," responded Bruno.

"He was strong. We needed him as leader. He did a lot of good for our country and for the other countries he took over as well. Ridding the world of Jews was exactly right. He saw the dirt in them, staining them. It's just a pity any of them survived." Sarah gave herself a shake at the thoughts in her mind. It was worrying her how much Bruno was changing. She didn't want to do anything to him but she might be given no choice if he continued like this. She refused to let him jeopardise herself and her new life.

Bruno said nothing just shook his head. There was no getting through to Sarah he realised. Would she let him cut all ties with her which was the way his current thoughts were going. He had loved her once but his feelings for her were fading more and more as time went on. He was becoming smitten with the Jew he was living with who was actually a much nicer person than Sarah was proving to be. He really didn't know what he saw in her.

He was constantly amazed at the human spirit. His Jewish partner was loving and kind, nothing like the scheming person he had been led to believe. She had been through so much in the camps but still hadn't lost who she essentially was. She had seen her family, including her children die at the hands of people like himself but still hadn't become hardened or bitter through it all. Of course he hadn't revealed his true identity to her and hoped he never would have to as he was sure he would see disappointment and disgust on her face. He respected her and was coming to love her so much that he didn't want to see it in her. He knew he was living a lie and she was falling in love with the person he presented not the real him who had done despicable things in the name of the Third Reich.

Bruno sincerely regretted the part he had played. He had been in charge of choosing who would live and who would die in Auschwitz Birkenau and at Bergen Belsen. It had been at Auschwitz he had met Sarah and fallen in love with her. He knew her to be violently opposed to the Jews which showed in her treatment of them and it seemed now when things had changed in their country she still felt the same. She was dangerous and he knew he wanted to get away from her, but didn't know how.

Sarah's face hardened as she looked at Bruno. "You better not be getting any ideas about leaving me or having a relationship with your Jew." She almost spat out the Jew word.

"It's up to me who I get involved with," he said quietly.

"Who says. I think you'll find it's me. Don't forget what I know about you."

"Do your worst, I'm past caring."

Sarah started to feel cold suddenly. She really was losing Bruno. If he really didn't care then she would be left with no choice as she wouldn't let herself get put in danger of capture.

"I think you'll find you do care. I won't let you go."

Bruno was worried. He knew he wanted to get away from her now she was threatening him. How could he do that. He knew she how dangerous she was and wouldn't hesitate to kill him if he wasn't careful. He had no wish to die, although he didn't know how to avoid it. If he gave himself up to the authorities that would probably be what would happen and if he tried to leave Sarah that's what would happen to him at her hands. He was in a no win situation. Death was the only option which he wanted to avoid.

He intended to give careful thought to his options when he went home to his lover. There had to be away around it, although he may have to tell the truth and let his lover do what she thought was best. It was a risk but he hoped she would forgive him and come up with ideas together about their future together.

....

Sarah was not in the best mood when she got home to find Jacob still sitting up waiting for her. He had only done this once before and she really didn't want to be seeing him tonight.

"Hello darling," said Jacob. He could see the look on her face and knew the evening hadn't gone well but he was determined to play the loving husband anyway.

"Don't darling me," she snapped.

"What's happened?"

"None of your business. Go to bed, I don't want to see your Jewish face."

Taken by surprise he went to his room. Although he suspected she was fully for the extermination of Jews this was the first time she had shown outward hostility. He lay awake wondering where to go from there. He had a feeling if only he could reach the dark recesses of his mind he would be able to identify her. She was starting to give herself away. He needed to escape but didn't know how to. It certainly couldn't be now as he would never get passed her. Also he couldn't do much with just one incident. Who would believe him anyway when the hospital had thought how loving she was. She was certainly good at taking people in as he was sure the doctors and the nurses were intelligent enough to see the truth if it were out there but they hadn't, they thought how wonderful and loving she was.

Sarah went to her own room, needing to think about her next move. She leaned under her bed and pulled out a box. Opening the box she took out the shiny looking gun and held it. She had a feeling she would need it before very long.

It had really upset her what Bruno had said. She was totally in love with him still but it seemed the Jewish woman had him fully in her grasp. He wasn't thinking clearly anymore which was worrying. She didn't want to have to use the gun on him but suspected that was what it would come down to in the end. If she lost complete control of him she would have two options to let him live but hand him over to the authorities or kill him. If she handed him over then she too would be at risk. She didn't want to lose him and kill him but didn't know the best way forward. He clearly no longer cared about her or the hold she had on him. If she truly had lost control the gun was the best option.

Holding the shining gun she turned it over and over in her hands, somewhat reverently. It was an instrument to be respected and to use sparingly. There were other ways of killing and she might have to consider those instead. If she were to shoot Bruno the authorities and the police would know it was murder and it would be more difficult to hide her guilt. Guns made a noise that was the problem.

She would not let danger close in on her. She would survive even if she lost her lovely Bruno. It really would be agonising if she had to take action against him. She still loved him and always had done since the first time she set eyes on him. Of course it had helped catching him out for helping the Jews and sparing the lives of some of those who were destined for the gas chambers. A war criminal, as they were now being called, he certainly was. She wasn't prepared to be hanged just because he changed his opinion. Getting rid of him would also make the Jew scum he was living with suffer as well which was all to the good. Could she lose Bruno though? Being of a selfish mindset she decided her safety had to come first and any way was he really her Bruno anymore. From what he was saying he was changing and falling in love with someone else which she just could not allow. He belonged to her.

The gun back in its box, she lay on the bed arms underneath her head thinking. Sarah really didn't know what to do for the best. Was it best to go along with Bruno for the time being. Make him think she was changing as well. At least that way she would get to keep him, at least she supposed she would. Was she really happy to sleep with Jacob though that was the real test. Certainly it would allay any doubts Jacob had as to her real identity if she were to do that. Well she could try it once anyway and see where it led. It would please Bruno and hopefully put off the day when he might leave her for his lover. Lover, was that really what the Jew now was? She, Sarah, was supposed to be that. Was she being replaced? If that were the case action would have to be taken. If she couldn't have Bruno then no one would.

CHAPTER NINE

Jacob opened his eyes and yawned. He was starting to stretch when he saw the figure lying in bed beside him with her eyes shut still fast asleep. He hadn't heard her come in. He was startled as she had never shown any interest in him at all since he had been home, not in that way anyway. All he usually saw was a sneer or distaste showing on her face.

He wanted to lean over, put his arm around her and kiss her but he didn't dare wake her. Maybe if he woke her he would discover it was all a dream as he certainly wasn't a prince in any fairy story. This was real life. Unless this was all a dream and he was about to wake up and find himself in the camps again. The way Sarah was treating him was just like being back there anyway so it wouldn't make much difference to him.

Jacob tried getting out of bed, being as quiet as he could and made his way to the kitchen. He liked his coffee in the mornings and he knew Sarah would like one. She always did so he would take her one through and they could sit up in bed drinking their coffee and chat. Maybe they could go out and do something during the day. It was a Saturday so she wouldn't be at work. Of course this was wishful thinking probably. His past life he supposed.

Sarah was still fast asleep when he went back with their coffees. He put it on the tiny bedside table next to her side of the bed so she could easily get to it when she woke up. Jacob got back into bed and took a sip of coffee. How he liked it first thing in the morning. It helped him wake up properly and always had done. That much hadn't changed since he was young. He supposed he was still young but he no longer felt it. He had been through too much, had seen too much to be young any longer.

He sat in bed looking across at Sarah. Like this he could see what he had fallen in love with. The lines on her face were very relaxed in sleep. He couldn't help himself, putting the cup down he leaned across her and smoothed the hair back from her face. She opened her eyes and looked at him.

"What do you think you're doing. Don't touch me."

"But….I…I thought you'd like it and you looked so beautiful, just how I remember you."

Sarah, now properly awake remembered her resolve to do as Bruno had suggested however distasteful it was to her.

She tried to smooth her features into a smile. "Of course I do. It was just a shock that's all," she said.

Jacob, however, had already pulled back and was drinking his coffee again.

Sarah saw her cup and picked it up, "Thank you sweetheart," she said with all the credibility she could muster.

"You've changed," commented Jacob.

"Not really, it's just taken a while to adjust to being free with my lovely husband again." What a good actress Sarah felt. She just hoped she could keep it up for the time being. Not for long just enough to convince him and Bruno that she was genuine.

"It's so good to have you back," said Jacob smiling at her.

"It's good to be back."

Sarah leaned across and pulled him into her arms. Jacob responded by putting his arms around her and kissing her cheek. He didn't want to rush her so he stuck to that for the moment. He needed to let Sarah take the lead and go at her pace.

For the first time since getting home he allowed himself to relax and think that he had been wrong and this was his Sarah after all. He didn't really know what she had been through and maybe he never would but it could have been worse than himself.

Sarah was thinking about Bruno. It was the only way she could cope with this intimacy with Jacob. Imagining she was in Bruno's arms in bed with him. What she had to do just to keep Bruno interested and to keep her safe. She just hoped Bruno would appreciate it and come back to her again. It was all for love of him and she wasn't prepared to lose him just yet. The time would come she was sure but she wasn't saying good bye until it was forced on her by circumstances.

....

"Good morning Evelyn my love," said Bruno on waking. He looked down on her with a smile on his face. A smile that lit up his eyes. He was totally smitten with her. He was sure he would never get fed up with the sight of her laying beside him. He could stay like that with her all day but this day was different. They were going to have to have a difficult conversation.

"You look serious," said Evelyn watching the smile fade from his face.

He nodded and said, "You know I was with Sarah last night, well she has me worried."

"In what way?"

"She knows how I feel about you and won't listen when I try and say you are human to. In fact she went as far as to threaten me. She has this hold over me because I helped some Jews in the camps avoid the gas chambers."

Evelyn shivered as the memories came flooding back.

"I'm sorry," said Bruno. "I don't want to make you remember what you'd rather forget."

There was silence between them for a few minutes before Evelyn began to laugh.

"What's so funny?" asked Bruno startled to say the least.

"It's…." she couldn't get the words out for laughing which was threatening to become hysteria.

"Come on snap out of it," said Bruno harshly. He didn't want to frighten her but needed her to calm down.

She recoiled at the sharpness of his tone. "Sorry, it's just that she hasn't got anything over you. Do I have to remind you that Nazism is over. In fact I'm sure if you were to be caught it would go better for you that you did try and help the Jews."

Bruno looked at her in wonder and slowly a smile spread across his face. "Of course you're right my darling. How could I not have realised?"

"You have been so tied to her and her views that you hadn't realised you were also free of her clutches."

"But she could still hurt me, or you for that matter."

"Only if we let her."

"You don't know her. She's dangerous. She's a true Nazi of the worst kind."

"Is there a worst kind?" asked Evelyn.

"You're probably right I was just thinking I'm not as bad as she is."

"We need to think this through carefully. There must be a way of getting you free of her clutches and start a new life with me."

"But how?"

"We could leave the country and move elsewhere. I think I would prefer that anyway. It would help get rid of the memories that threaten to engulf me at times."

"I can't leave the country. I would be recognised as belonging to the SS as it is stamped all over my papers. They would soon work out who I am."

Evelyn gave the matter some thought before saying, "We could move to the other side of the country. We don't have to stay here. She wouldn't know we had gone anywhere and wouldn't be able to find us."

Bruno grabbed her and kissed her full on the mouth. "You're a genius," he said.

She smiled at him. "I know I am. Seriously though, I think it's the best thing for us. We do need to get away from her clutches. A fresh start is what we need. Sarah, or whatever her real name is, is dangerous."

Bruno nodded. "I know she is. It's really hit home just how much so she is. That's great, I agree 100%. We haven't a chance of a relationship if we stay here."

"Why won't you tell me her real name?"

"It's better you don't know. That way if you should meet her you won't give anything away. It just seems safer."

Evelyn nodded. She trusted Bruno and accepted anything he said. She didn't know why she should really, as she was a Jew and he was a former member of the SS. He had changed though, she was certain of that. They went into each others arms and shared a long kiss until Evelyn broke it with a sigh.

"What was that about?"

"I'm just thinking how much I love you."

Bruno smiled down at her and kissed her again. "I love you so much as well. That's one thing Sarah did well. She brought the two of us together."

"I suppose we should thank her for it."

"Maybe not just yet," said Bruno.

"Never perhaps."

"That's more like it."

Bruno once again put his lips against Evelyn and kissed her. For a while he put Sarah and that problem out of his mind.

....

"I've just had a thought," said Evelyn.

"What?" asked Bruno, wondering what he would hear now. Evelyn had some strange ideas at times which made them both laugh.

"This time I'm being serious."

Bruno wiped the smile off his face and looked at her waiting, "Well you say Sarah could do anything even go as far as kill but what about us, surely we can do that as well. That would be another way of getting away from her. It would be permanent, never looking over our shoulders again. We could also rescue Jacob at the same time."

"I'm not sure," Bruno said slowly. "Knowing my luck she'd either survive or I'd get caught."

"There would be that risk yes, but wouldn't it be worth it?"

"I'll have a think but at the moment I'm not convinced."

"Surely there would be a way of committing murder that wouldn't be traced back to us or that could look accidental. It could even be seen as suicide considering that she was SS and wants to avoid getting caught."

"She's not the suicide type. She's very much into self preservation."

"No one would know that though. She's not in touch with anyone except you…."

"We don't know that," broke in Bruno. "She could communicate with other officers who still share her values and the values of the Third Reich."

"You've got a point there. Surely though if she were, one of them could have done the deed. They're all dangerous."

"It doesn't make sense."

Evelyn didn't say anything further on the subject but did file it away at the back of her mind for use if necessary at a later date. She did see where Bruno was coming from but thought there had to be a way around it. It was useless arguing though and she hated it. It reminded her of the guards shouting at them in the camps.

Bruno saw her withdraw into herself. "Heh," he said. "It's all right. I'll consider what you said. It would be something to think about at a later date if necessary. I'm not cross with you."

Evelyn nodded, unable to speak. Bruno wished he hadn't shown himself to be so anti killing Sarah. He had frightened his lover and he hated seeing her like that. She hadn't said much about what she went through but he knew how bad the camps had been so could imagine. He was sure it would be the same as the ones he'd worked in. He knew she hated raised voices. He could kick himself for raising his just now.

"Come on why don't we go out and have a walk in the park," said Bruno wanting to shake this mood from Evelyn.

Evelyn shook her head.

"Oh come on, it will be nice. It 's such a nice day outside. It's all right, you're perfectly safe. No one will stop you. Those days are gone remember."

"I know, but it's so hard to shake off that fear. It's always there."

Bruno hated himself at that moment. It was because of him and others like him that Evelyn was frightened of her own shadow. How had they let Hitler brainwash them into believing such rubbish? But it had happened and he wasn't proud of himself for taking part in the torture and death of so many Jews and other undesirables.

Bruno stood up and reached for her hand. She let him take it and stood up. "I'll be with you. I won't leave you so no one can hurt you with me by your side."

Evelyn gave a small nod. She supposed it was ok with Bruno with her. It was very rare for her to venture out these days and she only did it if Bruno was with her. Even so it took a huge amount of courage and she always felt as if she were looking over her shoulder for the first sign of danger.

Warily, Evelyn stepped outside their door and held tightly to Bruno's hand, not wanting to be separated from him.

"Let me have my hand. You'll squeeze the circulation out of it," said Bruno giving her a reassuring smile.

"Sorry," said a sheepish Evelyn.

"It's all right. I'll forgive you this time," he teased.

Evelyn smiled and relaxed slightly. She felt a bit silly but couldn't help it. She was scarred and damaged by all she had been through during those awful years. She didn't know if she would ever get over it or if the deep wounds were permanent. Although with Bruno at her side she felt safe. He would take care of her and wouldn't let anyone hurt her.

They had a quiet walk around the park and a sit down on a bench. Evelyn was reluctant at first remembering that Jews were not allowed to sit on public benches in case the Aryan population were to catch some awful disease from them. It was hard to put years of discrimination and torture behind her. She was lucky to have found such an understanding and loving man in Bruno.

They were sat quietly talking and minding their own business with Evelyn quite relaxed by now and enjoying being with her lover. Suddenly out of nowhere a dog started barking and running towards them. Evelyn screamed and stood up ready to run. Although she knew she would never outrun the dog.

"It's ok," said Bruno, "It won't hurt you."

"They've come for me."

"There's no one just a dog trying to be friendly."

"I'm so sorry," said an elderly gentleman walking hurriedly towards them. "He likes to make friends with everyone he meets. He won't hurt you miss, he just wants a fuss made of him and to play that's all. He doesn't even bark when anyone comes to the door."

"It's all right," said Bruno. "My girlfriend has had a bad experience with dogs."

"Oh I'm sorry to hear that," said the elderly man. "Fluff come here, that's it good dog." The dog moved away from the couple and went to his owner wagging his tail madly.

Unfortunately this encounter ruined the day for them as Evelyn became tense and twitchy again, on high alert for danger, even one that didn't exist.

Bruno hated seeing her like this and wondered if she would ever change. He knew inside it was early days yet. It was only a few months that she had been free so it would take time.

"I'm sorry," said Evelyn when they got back to the safety of her own four walls.

"You've nothing to apologise for," said Bruno. "Maybe it was wrong of me to push you into going."

"No it's not that. It was good to be out. I just couldn't cope with the dog. It brought back memories of the dogs at the camp who always snarled at us as if we were their next meal."

"I know and I do understand," said Bruno in a gentle voice. "I'm just so very sorry for my part in it. I'll never be able to atone for what I did. I know now how wrong I was. Even back then I knew it was wrong and started to feel very uncomfortable but there was no way out for me. I was in the SS and that was that. My life would have been over if I had made it known that I didn't like what was happening."

"I do understand you know," said Evelyn quietly. "I'm just glad that not everyone was evil during that time. There was good amongst the evil although it wasn't always obvious."

Bruno put his arm around Evelyn, "I found you and that has to be a good thing out of all that was bad. I do love you."

"I know and I love you to." She gave a bit of a laugh.

"What's funny?"

"I was just thinking that we make an unlikely couple. Just a few months ago we were enemies and now look at us, lovers sharing a bed."

"You're right."

The two lovers went into each others arms and shared a special time together, each thankful for having found love in the darkest of places.

CHAPTER TEN

Jacob looked across at Sarah who was sat with her head in the newspaper. A frown had crossed her face which had caught Jacob's eye.

"You all right love?""

"Hmm, yes, yes it's nothing. Sorry."

"That's ok. Is it bad news?"

"No just something that has brought memories up again. Apparently the authorities are trying to capture members of the SS who were involved in the prison camps. They want to put u…. them before a war crimes tribunal."

Sarah was aware she had nearly tripped up there. She had so nearly revealed her secret to Jacob and if she did that would be the end. Fortunately he didn't seem to notice her stumbling over the words, or if he did he didn't connect it with anything. She really was going to have to be more careful. She was still taking the advice Bruno had given her about sleeping with Jacob and trying to be nice to him. It stuck in her throat but she did it just to make it more authentic. She had noticed over that time that Jacob was now more relaxed and more accepting of her which was a good thing. It meant he wasn't likely to guess anything were amiss. She didn't know how much longer she could keep it up for though. It wasn't easy pretending to be someone she wasn't.

Jacob relaxed back in his chair smiling inwardly. He had stopped thinking this wasn't his Sarah now that she was coming around. He decided it had just been connected with what she had been through and not wanting to hurt him while he was so traumatised. There was just one problem remaining and that was Sarah still wouldn't let him outside, either alone or with her. He had been so happy to have his Sarah back that he hadn't broached the subject yet. He knew that before long he would have to say something. He was starting to go stir crazy stuck in the house all day every day, especially during the week when Sarah was at work. She still went out in the evenings a few times a week and still hadn't told him where she went at those times. He worried because he was getting dark early now and he didn't like her to be alone. Anything could happen to a woman on her own. She had insisted she could look after herself, that no one could hurt her in a way she hadn't already been hurt. She had been through the worst of mans inhumanity to man she insisted and no one could harm her now.

....

Sarah was fed up with the way things were working out, or should say wasn't working out. She couldn't keep going pretending to have a love for Jacob that wasn't there. Things with Bruno weren't great either. He still met with her but no longer seemed to be on her wavelength and was reluctant to sleep with her anymore. She felt his withdrawal badly but didn't know what to do about it.

"What's wrong?" she asked him on one occasion.

"Oh, nothing," he replied.

"You've become very quiet of late. Something must be bothering you."

"No it's not honestly."

"I should polygraph you that will find out the truth," she said half jokingly.

"You don't want to know my dark secrets," he said without thinking.

"Dark secrets, now what might they be as I already have something I can use if you try and get away from us."

"Nothing, not really, just a figure of speech. I didn't mean anything by it."

Bruno shook himself. He wasn't paying much attention and came close to admitting his relationship with Evelyn which had taken on new proportions lately. He needed to be more careful as he was aware of how frustrated Sarah was becoming. Her pretending to be the woman Jacob loved was taking its toll on her. She wanted to go back to the way she was originally even though Bruno said it was better to carry on this way as it would arouse less suspicion.

She had agreed but complained every time she saw him. She blamed him for having to give way so much when all she really wanted to do was torture the Jewish scum. It was all he deserved.

She had thoroughly relished her role in the camp and loved nothing better than cracking that whip against people who started slacking. Sending people to the gas chambers was even more fun in her eyes. Deep down she was a sadist and she recognised that in herself. Love didn't exist in her eyes except for Bruno who had somehow managed to creep into her affections.

....

"Why can't I go outside?" asked Jacob the next day. She had seemed in a better mood and he thought was the best time to bring the subject up.

"You won't cope with it. It's for your own good. To protect you from people who could hurt and bully you."

"Don't you think that's up to me to decide. I've been through so much I don't think anything worse could happen now. I'm safe, we're safe. Nazism is over. Besides you go out regularly without a problem."

That's what you think, thought Sarah to herself. It's not over while I have breath in my body. There were others who still felt the same. Of course she couldn't tell Jacob that. She had to make up excuses that weren't holding water evidently as he still tried to persuade her to change her mind.

"Why can't we go out together then. I admit I would feel safer knowing you were by my side."

"What use do you think I would be if anything were to happen. I'm only a woman, a Jewish woman at that."

"From what you have said and what I learnt in hospital religion no longer matters. We are accepted now. No yellow star, no special laws prohibiting us from breathing. So it's perfectly safe to go out."

Sarah stayed quiet not sure how to respond. It was looking like she would have to let him out at some point in the near future just to keep him quiet but it scared her. Giving him more independence could be tricky. There would be nothing stopping him from telling the authorities about her. Bruno would be no use either as she didn't like the way things were going there either.

Sarah conceded defeat, "Ok we'll go for a stroll at the weekend together. Not long mind you. I don't want you struggling again. I'm so pleased you are feeling so much better. Have any more memories come back yet."

Jacob shook his head, there was no change and he didn't think there would be. This relieved Sarah greatly and left her feeling safer now. she gave a rather insincere smile at her lover before turning away to prevent him from seeing the look of pure hatred on her face and in her eyes. He was so sensitive she couldn't risk him picking up on anything. He wouldn't tell her if he did as he still kept very much to himself. She had never heard about the content of the regular nightmares he still had. She was fast running out of patience at the disturbed nights but Bruno insisted it wasn't surprising. No one could go through all that and survive unscathed.

Jacob no longer relished the hours she was at work. He found the days long and boring with nothing to do. He wanted to be able to use his brain on something but there was no outlet. All he could do was sit down twiddling his thumbs. Sarah wouldn't even leave him the papers to read on the basis it would be too traumatic for him. He felt she was being too over protective but she insisted and he didn't want to aggravate the situation. It was too volatile. It still worried him that there were handcuffs on the bed. Although Sarah had improved in her attitude towards him he still didn't quite trust her. Things still didn't add up. He had got no further forward in discovering who she was and had given up for awhile.

....

It was the middle of the afternoon and Jacob was laying on the bed having a rest. He still needed that time during the day as he got very tired and on edge quickly. On this occasion thoughts were going round and round in his head. They were primarily over Sarah's real identity of which he was no nearer discovering. She was a good actress he had to admit. Although he had given her the benefit of the doubt and accepted she was who she said she was, he wasn't convinced. There were still things that didn't add up which included not being allowed out. He longed for fresh air but didn't get any. Even the windows were kept locked so he couldn't breathe in any from that source.

If he did discover who she was he wondered how he would be able to free himself from the relationship and tell someone what was going on. What would he say anyway? Sarah was sleeping with him now, no that wasn't going to convince anyone, he would just get funny looks and he would deserve it. He could of course, deliberately set her off which would ruin the closeness she allowed. It would unleash her fury which he felt was just under the surface and set her off treating him badly again.

Jacob couldn't even be sure that there was anything to tell but instinct told him she was trouble and that she could be dangerous. He needed to find out more and then find a way of reporting her. He knew deep inside that was what he had to do but he was patient. He could wait until the time came. In the meantime he would go along with her and try and push her to loosen the reins a bit. He would have to know where to go when the time came that he needed to get help.

At the same time Jacob was thinking about this he was also giving thought to her being Sarah, his beloved wife. He was a mass of contradictions and didn't know what was truth or lies. He had no one he could trust to talk to who might be able to put it into perspective for him. He really needed friends. He didn't know what had become of his friends during the war years. His Jewish friends could have perished and most likely had, and his other friends, well anything could have happened.

Jacob closed his eyes to try and sleep but he was too on edge. He had to get outside, but short of breaking a window didn't know how. He somehow had to persuade Sarah to go with him.

Claustrophobia was setting in badly. His breathing became more rapid and the room started swirling around and round in circles. He gripped the side of the bed with a tight hold to avoid finding himself on the floor. He didn't know which was best, eyes closed or open, he tried both but neither helped at all. He was panting hard, struggling to breathe and becoming frightened with each shallow breath he took. Was he dying? This had never happened to him before, not even in those early days in the hospital.

The next thing he knew was Sarah knelt on the floor beside the bed holding his hand.

"It's ok. You're going to be fine. It was just a panic attack. You poor love you really are badly traumatised aren't you, but you're safe now."

"What happened?" asked Jacob, still quite groggy.

"You had a panic attack and must have passed out."

"I remember gripping the side of the bed because it felt as if I was going to fall out."

"Do you know what triggered it? Talking about it might help."

"I was thinking how much I hate being stuck indoors day in day out. I long to be out in the fresh air. Also I was wondering what happened to my friends."

Sarah thought quickly for something to say without giving herself away. Jacob however, sensed the pause and wondered what it meant.

"Ok look, later when it starts getting dark we'll go out for a brief walk. Just to the end of the road and back."

"Can't we go now? Surely it would be better in daylight."

"You don't want people pointing you out and attacking you do you."

"Why would they do that? I was told I'm safe now and the camps have been emptied."

"There are still people who live in the past. Too many Nazis still exist unfortunately."

Jacob was quiet, taking this in. He didn't know whether to believe it or not. He would have to accept it for now though because she was all he had. His freedom was in her hands. When outside he could assess the situation and decide how easy it would be to get away from her. Although male he knew he was still weakened from the hunger and disease that was rife in the camps. She could be stronger than himself and probably was. She didn't look as if she had been starved.

"Do you think you can get up now? We could go through to the kitchen to make something to eat then we'll go out."

Jacob stood up, trying not to appear too eager. He clung on to Sarah still feeling a bit wobbly.

"Are you sure you'll be able to go out? You're not very steady at the moment."

"I'll be fine, I probably just need something to eat," he said.

Sarah nodded, but was thinking she could use this to prevent him from leaving the house. After all there would be some truth in it she genuinely didn't want him falling over. She felt that the real Sarah would say the same thing.

Jacob proved right, after eating a couple of slices of toast he was back to his normal self. Sarah no longer had any excuses to keep him locked away.

"You'll need your coat on, it's getting quite chilly in the evenings," said Sarah.

Jacob, when they left the house was well wrapped up, warm coat, hat, scarf and gloves. He felt this was a bit of an exaggeration but went along with it. Sure enough when he stepped outside he felt a bitter chill in the air. Totally out of proportion from the warm house he was used to.

He clung on to Sarah, feeling anxiety taking hold of him again.

"Do you want to turn back? Maybe it's too soon for you to venture out."

"I'll be fine. I've got to do it sometime. I can't stay hidden away forever."

He will if I have any say in the matter, thought Sarah, but at the same time smiled and agreed with him with a nod of her head.

Sarah was getting out of her depth she now acknowledged. As Jacob got stronger he was more demanding and she didn't know how to restrain him without making him suspicious. She thought of the handcuffs she'd had ready but didn't want to use them or anything else because that would cause him to think again. She didn't want him to work anything out in his mind. She wondered about talking to Bruno but decided against it. He was definitely changing and she wasn't sure what to do about that except to use her gun. He was still useful to her so she kept him alive for the time being, although she didn't have the control over him she'd had originally.

She knew Bruno would be all for letting Jacob out sometimes. During her surveillance of Bruno she knew he was going out with his rotten Jew and worse still he had kissed her openly in public. How gross that was. She'd almost been sick at the sight. It had put her off kissing him herself as she didn't want to catch anything he might have caught from his Jew.

She had to be careful when following Bruno because he would spot her easily if he became suspicious. She had gained good skills from the SS and he would have the same. If she wasn't careful he would pick up that he was being followed.

Contrary to what she told Jacob she wasn't really working. She was following Bruno to see what he was doing and she knew he was getting too close to his partner which hadn't been part of the plan. She thought the time was right to carry her gun just in case she needed to use it. She didn't really want to use it out in the open in case anyone spotted her but she would need some excuse.

In her malicious mind Bruno needed to know what she was doing before she did it. She wanted him to feel the fear of God in him as she took aim and fired.

Sarah had been an ideal choice for the SS. She had been hand selected due to her sadism. She had often interviewed Jews and suspected resistance workers and knew just how far to go with torture techniques. She relished these times. It was what she missed most about the SS. It was a good feeling keeping control of Jacob but she knew that would wear off soon and she would be unable to resist using torture on him.

Back at home Jacob collapsed into a chair with a look of exhaustion over his face.

"You're tired now. Why don't you rest?" suggested Sarah.

"Mmm," said Jacob too tired to even speak a sentence.

He stood up and made his way to his room. He never presumed anything so stayed away from her room. Anyway it was his room she went to at night if she wanted to sleep with him which she did most nights.

Sarah had no intention of going to him this time though. She wanted to think about her next move. She wondered about getting someone to approach Jacob while they were out and insult him and possibly beat him up lightly. The problem being her acquaintances had either been arrested or had disappeared off the radar just as she had done. She had never had any friends and Bruno was the closest anyone had got to her. She couldn't ask him though knowing now that he wouldn't agree.

She thought through carefully wondering if she could get away with it herself without Jacob knowing. She wouldn't be able to insult him though she would only be able to be physically harming. Not only that but behind him. It wouldn't work that well though as he would never think it could be because of his Jewishness. The more she thought the more excited she became. How she would enjoy watching. She of course, would be an innocent bystander and pretending to be a target as well.

She could always hire a thug. There were always plenty of them around. Yes, she might have to do that. It would have to be a prearranged time when there weren't many people around to see and get suspicious. She would have to arrange it but first must think carefully as to the time of day. It had been very quiet with as few a people as possible in case any tried to rescue or prevent it in someway.

Sarah found just the person she was looking for. He was very muscular and said he had done a lot of boxing in the past. She wasn't allowed to know his name and wouldn't be able to contact him. He said it was for his and her safety.

"When do you want me to do it? Night would be best," he said.

"That should be all right. How about tonight. I can make sure Jacob is out for a walk during that time. You'll spot us quite easily. I'll run away fairly early on so I don't compromise myself. Don't kill him and don't do enough damage that he ends up in hospital again."

"You're weird, do you know that," said the man. He was slightly afraid of her but wasn't going to admit to it.

"It's just to encourage him to stay indoors in future. It isn't in my interests for him to be outside."

"I think it best I don't know who you are either. I'm not altogether comfortable with this job. Usually there is a good reason for beating someone up but you haven't been able to supply me with a suitable one yet."

Sarah was worried. Had she chosen wrongly? She didn't think so, he really did look the part but he asked too many questions and that was just what she didn't want.

"We agreed no questions asked," she reminded him.

"I know but I always like a certain amount of background information."

"You don't answer my questions so you should respect me as well," Sarah said.

He acknowledged this and when he had received half the payment up front they parted going their separate ways without another word.

Sarah couldn't wait for the time to take Jacob out again. They had been doing it for a few days now and Jacob was getting more confident as time went on. She was doing the right thing she had no doubt. It would make him more dependent on her and more likely to refuse to go out again.

....

"Let's go for a walk again. You're getting so confident these days it's great."

Jacob went straight for his jacket without saying a word. He didn't have to, the grin that lit up his face said it all. Sarah remained grim but he was too excited to notice.

They were walking near their home when suddenly there was a lot of noise coming from behind. Jacob half turned, scared. He gripped Sarah's hand tighter. There were two men rushing at them shouting at him.

"Here look what we've got. He has to be a filthy Jew. What's he doing here? We need to teach him a lesson he won't forget," said one of the men whom Sarah didn't recognise.

They grabbed Jacob, snatching him away from Sarah who just stood there with a look of horror on her face. She was acting for all she was worth, not wanting this to come back to her in case anyone was around and witnessed the beating.

Jacob was thrown to the ground and then the kicking started. He pulled his knees up to his chest in an effort to protect himself but to no avail. The kicks and punches continued. They were careful to avoid his head as per the agreement with Sarah.

"What are you looking at? Do you want the same thing? We could have something better lined up for you," said the man known to Sarah.

"P…please no," said Sarah pretending to be very afraid.

"Aww come on. You know you want it. I bet this piece of dirt doesn't satisfy your need," cajoled the other man.

Sarah shook her head. The fear was starting to become real as she realised the other man meant what he said. Her being attacked wasn't part of the bargain. She hadn't signed up for that.

The man said, "Oh come on. We're wasting our time here. Who wants someone sleeping with a Jew anyway. Bet we'd catch something."

The men went on their way and Sarah breathed a sigh of relief. She bent over Jacob who was giving small moans of pain. She spoke to him but he didn't respond.

"Jacob, Jacob," she called, but nothing. There was no sign that he had heard her.

"Help! Help!" she called.

No one came. It didn't really surprise her as this was a rough area and everyone kept to themselves not wanting to get involved with anything. Beatings were common, it's why she had chosen it. Right now she wished someone would respond as she was frightened by his silence. She didn't know if he was conscious or not. He wasn't supposed to be badly injured but she was afraid that's what had happened.

She knelt by his side repeating his name and telling him he was safe.

"Is everything ok, can I help," said a voice coming from above her.

She looked up to see a kind face looking down at her.

"Please help," she said through the tears. "It's my husband. He was grabbed and beaten up."

"It's all right. I'm a nurse," said the lady. "My name is Ingrid by the way. You're lucky, I don't usually come this way on my way home from work. I just fancied a change today."

"I'm so glad you did."

"Well, let's see what's going on here. What's his name?"

"Jacob."

"Jacob can you hear me. Squeeze my hand if you can." There was something, only very slight but better than nothing.

Ingrid looked at Sarah and smiled, "I'm sure he'll be ok he gripped my hand slightly. It's not much but means he can hear even if he can't respond as yet."

"Oh thank God! Thank God!" cried Sarah.

Ingrid did a few checks. "His pulse is good. I'm sure he'll come round properly in a short while. He should go to hospital to get checked out though. He could have broken ribs, internal bleeding anything."

"Surely not. I….this is all my fault. I knew I shouldn't let him come out for a walk with me."

"Why? You couldn't have predicted this."

"He's a Jew."

"That's not a problem anymore. They are just human beings like the rest of us."

"We know that but there are still thugs around who want any excuse."

Ingrid nodded. "I think you need to call the police as well."

"I can't do that. If they discover I've informed on them they'll come after me."

"I'm sure they won't. You are probably just a random couple who happened to be in the wrong place at the wrong time," said Ingrid. She was trying to reassure Sarah but could see she was failing.

Sarah was no longer acting, her fear had become all to real and she didn't like it. She was also worried Ingrid might say something to the police and she didn't want anyone looking at her.

"Ahh," Jacob let out a loud groan and opened his eyes. "What happened?" he whispered.

"You were beaten up. I'm Ingrid by the way, I'm a nurse and happened to be passing."

"Sarah?" he asked.

"Yes I'm here. Everything will be ok. They didn't touch me."

"I'm so glad. It's my fault I'm in this mess. I should have listened to you and stayed at home where I was safe."

Ingrid was about to respond when she caught the look on Sarah's face. Something wasn't right here. Sarah had already told her she persuaded him to come out but Jacob was contradicting that. What was really going on? she wondered.

"Let's get you home," said Sarah putting an arm around Jacob who was sitting up by this time.

"I really would advise against that. He needs to be checked over in hospital," said Ingrid.

"Poof to that. I can look after him better at home. He'll be happier and more settled there in familiar surroundings."

Ingrid couldn't respond to that but was still concerned.

"Come on love, can you get to your feet?" asked Sarah.

Sarah was trying to put her acting skills to use again and convince Ingrid that everything was ok and that she was just a concerned wife.

Ingrid took the other side and together they helped Jacob get to his feet.

"Don't rush," said Ingrid. "Stand still for a minute or two while your head settles down."

Sarah tried not to show her impatience, but Ingrid being a sensitive soul picked up on it anyway. There wasn't much she missed.

"Right come on then let's get you home and to bed."

Jacob nodded briefly until a stab of pain stopped him. Ingrid noticed and said, "He's in pain, he really needs to be checked by a doctor."

"No, he'll be fine once he's at home in bed. There is no need for anything. I'm sure he's just badly bruised."

"I hope so," said a sceptical Ingrid. "But at least let me help you get him home and settled."

"No, no need for that. I can manage. He's a lightweight really," said Sarah hurriedly. No way did she want any interfering busybodies nosing around where they weren't wanted.

"Well if you're sure," said a reluctant Ingrid.

It was obvious that Sarah wanted nothing from her for whatever reason of her own. She turned away bidding the couple good bye.

Ingrid walked off in the opposite direction lost in thought. Something odd was going on there. It seemed strange they had assaulted Jacob but left Sarah alone. What was even more odd was Sarah's insistence on not getting help for Jacob. If she loved Jacob as much as she said she did then she would be worried sick and want to know that Jacob really was ok. Why was Sarah so concerned that Ingrid didn't know where they lived? Something was definitely wrong. She needed to visit them at home and take them by surprise one day, but that was difficult when she didn't know and wasn't allowed to know where they lived which was just a bit weird.

Ingrid made a decision to turn back and try to find them and follow where they went. It shouldn't be too difficult to find them as they weren't going to be making fast progress with Jacob as injured as he was. He had been all bent over when they turned away to go home.

Sure enough Ingrid soon saw them in the distance. She slowed her pace not wanting to give herself away. She didn't want to arouse any suspicions in the couple. She was sure Jacob at least would be twitchy, listening for footsteps. He would definitely be on high alert. She watched them turn a corner into a cul de sac. That must be where they lived, thought Ingrid. She stopped at the corner and peered her head slightly round it. She saw the couple stop and Sarah reach into her bag and pull out what looked like keys. The door opened and they disappeared inside.

Creeping around the corner a few minutes later she walked stealthily along the road to see if she could work out which house they had gone into. She stopped half way down and decided that was probably the one she thought.

If she were right she would have to be careful and try and begin a friendship with Jacob when he was alone. She, of course had no inkling of what was happening just suspicions to go on. She would have to make some excuse for turning up unannounced.

．．．．．．．．．

Sarah was trying to get Jacob to bed but with difficulty. She wanted him on his side but he insisted he lay on his back, which was the usual position. He would lay on his back as best he could. What he was finding hard to understand was why Sarah refused to allow Ingrid to help as she had offered.

Sarah started to get impatient with Jacob. He couldn't be as bad as he was making out. Yes she had been worried at first but was reassured when he started coming round. She had in her own way been grateful for Ingrid's input in letting her know he would be ok even though she wouldn't let her help further or take him to hospital.

"I think I had better sleep in the other room tonight," she said. "I don't want to hurt you when I turn over in the night."

"I'll be fine. I'm tougher than you think. I survived the death camps so I have to be."

Sarah didn't like hearing this. It meant she hadn't achieved her objective by paying someone to beat him up. He still showed a fighting spirit instead of becoming dependent on her. If she wasn't careful she could lose him and that wasn't an option. She may have to go back to the way she was at the beginning and ignore Bruno's advice.

CHAPTER ELEVEN

"I really think you have to continue as you have been," said Bruno on hearing the story. In his mind he was concerned that Sarah might have engineered this plan although she hadn't said as much. It seemed she was becoming cagey around him. That could be a bad or a good thing depending on her thinking. He hoped it was good because that would mean she was moving away from him emotionally and leaving him more to his own devices. If however, there was distrust building inside her it could be dangerous for him and he may have to disappear sooner than anticipated. He and Evelyn would have to discuss this situation that had arisen and take it from there. He was grateful for Evelyn's help as she was wise beyond her years. She had to be to survive the horrors she had experienced and witnessed.

"But if he's not becoming dependent on me then I'll have to make him so."

"Not by torture you won't. You'll just frighten him and make him want to escape."

"He won't be able to as I'll use those handcuffs and chain him to the bed."

"You can't do that," said a horrified Bruno.

"And why not."

"He'll know for sure something is wrong and will be looking for ways to get out. You'll be giving yourself away."

"There will be no escape if he's in handcuffs. He doesn't know anyone or meet anyone so I think I'll be safe."

Bruno shook his head. She really was a hard case. He didn't know what he'd originally seen in her. A diehard Nazi that's what she was. He had reached the point where he kept making excuses not to sleep with her. He would like to avoid seeing her but he hadn't perfected reasons not to as yet. Evelyn had tried to help there but none were acceptable for her ladyship Sarah.

Bruno sighed inwardly. If he knew where she and Jacob were living he would have been very tempted to get Jacob out of there as soon as could possibly be arranged. He would tell Jacob who she really was and take him to the authorities to hand her in. He said as much to Evelyn when he got home having escaped Sarah's clutches. He feared for Jacob though.

"You could always follow Sarah one evening and see where she goes. It should lead you to the general area where they are living even if you can't get the actual address."

Bruno thought for a moment before saying, "You're a genius do you know that." He scooped her off her feet and kissed her on the lips.

"That's why you love me," she said trying to sound modest.

"Big head," he said starting to laugh.

"Of course."

They stayed in each others arms for what seemed like forever. Only pulling apart when Evelyn suggested she should make them something to eat.

"Are you sure. I have other ideas."

"Naughty, naughty," said Evelyn going back into his arms.

Bruno led her into the bedroom and they both fell on the bed.

Much later Evelyn awoke and propped up on one elbow she looked down at the man she had come to love very much. She wished she could resolve the Sarah situation as she was the one blot on their life together. She was also one very dangerous individual.

"You know something, I've made a decision I'm going to do as you suggested and follow Sarah next time I see her. I think she goes straight home so I should be able to find it easily enough."

"Good for you," said Evelyn, "But be careful. I don't want you to get hurt or worse still killed. I love you too much."

"Do you really?" asked an incredulous Bruno.

"I do," she said her face radiant with happiness.

"I feel the same but I didn't dare hope you would feel it too."

"You mean you thought I would sleep with anyone because I'm a Jew and a prostitute." She turned away from him not wanting him to see the hurt in her eyes.

"I didn't mean it like that," he said pulling her back to face him. He saw tears in her eyes. "I mean that I'm glad you feel the same."

She pulled away again.

He said, "That didn't help did it. I'm just digging myself deeper into that hole aren't I."

Evelyn nodded, then turned to face him laughter in her eyes. "I was worried you wouldn't feel like that about me. It took a lot of courage to admit how I feel about you."

"I know," said Bruno gently.

"We just have to work together to help Jacob and get that woman out of his life and out of ours."

Bruno nodded and said, "I couldn't agree more. But I'll start tomorrow and follow her after we say goodbye."

"Sounds a good plan."

"You would think so, after all it was your idea."

"True. I think I'll have to give my halo a polish," she said, laughter bubbling up inside.

………..

Bruno turned to leave Sarah after a brief goodnight kiss that was becoming more and more one sided. He started walking off in the opposite direction as if headed for home. He turned and to his surprise she was stood still watching him go. He raised his hand with a smile which wasn't returned. It was only when he had turned a corner he tried looking back. She was gone, but in what direction. She could be anywhere. That plan had failed then. He continued his walk home when he felt a tap on the shoulder. He jumped wondering who it could be. He felt frightened sure it had something to do with Sarah.

"Sorry to frighten you," said a female voice.

"Okay. Who are you? What do you want?"

"My name's Ingrid. I'm a nurse who helped when Jacob was beaten up."

"Oh I know, Sarah told me about you. What can I do for you?" he asked still puzzled on being approached in this way.

"I wanted to know what you know about the situation. I think Jacob could be in trouble. Things just didn't add up."

"How do I know you are genuine?"

"Meet me at the hospital tomorrow lunchtime then you can ask anyone you want. I'm a nurse there. We'll talk then."

"Great will do. Is it all right if I bring a friend?"

"Of course," said Ingrid.

The two said goodbye with a handshake and they went their separate ways.

Arriving home, Bruno was excited which got Evelyn wondering.

"What's happened?" she asked. "You don't usually look like that after meeting Sarah."

"You'll never believe what happened."

"You saw Jacob and rescued him?"

"Don't be silly. I don't think it will be as simple as that."

"I suppose not but I could live in hope. Stranger things have happened."

"No I had a chat with a lady called Ingrid."

"As in the nurse who helped when Jacob was beaten up."

"The very same."

"Wow I can't believe it. What does she want?"

"Our help apparently."

"You mean she has guessed something is wrong and wants to help rescue Jacob."

"I think so. We are meeting her at the hospital tomorrow for lunch."

"Wow. Great news. No wonder you look so excited. This might be the break we are looking for."

"I know."

Neither of them slept much that night. The situation was going round and round in their heads. They were both tossing and turning but said little until Evelyn gave up on sleep and put the light on.

She sat up in bed asking if he wanted a hot chocolate, thinking that might help them sleep. He nodded but said nothing.

"I still can't help wondering if we're walking into a trap here. She could be one of Sarah's mates."

"Isn't that why we're meeting at the hospital, so we can verify her credentials?"

"I suppose so. I'm just being stupid aren't I."

"I don't think so. You're just being cautious which is a good thing in this situation. I'm sure Ingrid will have understood if she is the person I think she is."

....

"Are you ready," called Bruno for the third time. "We really must leave now or she'll be finished her lunch break and we'll have achieved nothing."

"I'm just coming."

"That's what you said ten minutes ago," he said sounding exasperated now. Women, he thought. How does it take them so long. They were all the same.

At that moment Evelyn came down the stairs.

"How did it take that long when you're dressed so casually?" he asked.

"I dress carefully. I don't just bundle things on like you do."

Bruno shook his head. "Come on we'll have to rush now."

The couple quickly made their way to the hospital. They had to ask for directions to the café where Bruno saw Ingrid waiting for them.

"Hello, can we join you? This is Evelyn by the way. She's my partner."

"Pleased to meet you." Ingrid held out her hand to shake Evelyn's.

"What is it you want to know?" asked Bruno coming straight to the point. He didn't see any reason to waste time with pleasantries.

"You're certainly very direct."

"I don't see any reason for small talk when we need to get down to the serious stuff."

"I'm worried about Jacob."

"You are aware we don't know Jacob directly."

"Oh I didn't realise that as you seemed such a close friend of Sarah's."

"Not so close anymore. But I'll help if I can."

"I want to know everything you know about Sarah and their life together."

Bruno looked around before saying anything. He needed to make sure no one would overhear them. He still couldn't be sure if this was a trap which could lead to danger for him and Evelyn.

"It's ok no one can hear anything. Everyone is minding their own business. If we talk quietly we'll be fine. I'm safe I can assure you. It's Jacob I'm worried about."

Bruno began the story starting at the beginning and continued until the end.

"Wow that's some story."

Bruno nodded. He had been quite open about who he was as well as he felt it was needed. He didn't know why but somehow he trusted her to do the best she could for Jacob. They were allies for now.

"I can at least tell you where they live, having followed Sarah home that evening."

"I found out getting him beaten up didn't have any effect. He's still as keen to go out and get to know people."

"Hmm, that could mean trouble for Jacob."

"We know," said Evelyn speaking for the first time.

"I think maybe we should go to see Jacob when we know Sarah isn't there. She is quite predictable about her routine."

"It might be best for you both to go and leave me to distract Sarah. I'll be due to see her anyway so I'll just keep her talking longer or something, anything to prevent her meeting you both."

"Sounds a good plan. Do you feel up to this?" asked Ingrid, turning to Evelyn who nodded her approval.

"How about we do this tonight. You'll be seeing her then won't you?" Evelyn asked Bruno.

Bruno nodded.

Ingrid said, "If we hide behind some trees we'll watch for Sarah approaching. When she does we'll be off. It will give us longer with Jacob."

"Are you planning on getting him out tonight?" asked Bruno.

Ingrid shook her head, "I don't think so. We'll hopefully tell him what the situation is and try and sus out Sarah's daily routine."

"Great," said Evelyn.

"Anyway I must get back to work," said Ingrid standing up.

Bruno and Evelyn stayed where they were and watched their new friend disappear back to the wards.

"She seems nice," said Evelyn.

Bruno nodded but kept quiet.

"Earth to Bruno. What are you thinking?"

"I'm just thinking about tonight. I don't like the thought of involving you. It's too dangerous if Sarah catches you."

"I'll be all right. Careful is my middle name. I'm a survivor don't forget."

"I don't know what I'd do if I lost you."

"You won't lose me. I'm not going anywhere without you."

"You don't know how dangerous Sarah is if she's crossed."

"I think I do. I've met her sort before in the form of guards in the camps. A sadistic bunch on the whole. Also you have said enough to make me suspect how violent she could be."

"I'll do my bit and try as hard as I can to keep her as long as possible."

"That's all we can do, our best."

CHAPTER TWELVE

"I've so missed you," said Bruno.

Sarah snuggled up closer to her man and smiled. Maybe things were looking up and Bruno had realised where he was well off. She had been right to just go with the flow and see what happened. That Jew, whoever she was, was now out of favour. He'd come to his senses without her having to take action.

Bruno saw the smile and tried not to set his face too grimly. She obviously thought she had him back. She'd be in for a shock soon when Jacob disappeared. He knew it wouldn't be that evening but they were well on the way to making it happen.

He tightened his hold on Sarah and started exploring her body with his hands. Yes Sarah was responding that was good. It meant the two women would have longer to find Jacob and make contact. There was no talking necessary, they were just two lovers well acquainted with each other. Their bodies moulded together as one.

It was with reluctance Bruno pulled away. He felt the play acting had to come to an end and he must go home to his real love. She should be back by then unless anything had gone desperately wrong.

It suddenly occurred to him that Jacob might tell his so called wife about the visit of the two women, then they would all be in for it. Who knew what Sarah would do if crossed. He didn't know about the gun she had hidden away but he knew it would be bad and probably involve violence of some sort. This hadn't occurred to any of them when making their plans. He hoped to God – whom he didn't believe in - that it would work out well for all their sakes.

…………..

Bruno once at home was on tenterhooks wondering what had happened. He started to worry because Evelyn wasn't there. He was worried they would get caught. The plan hadn't been meant to take so long. Had something gone wrong? Had they had to free Jacob there and then because of the situation they found him in. There were so many different scenarios and they were all playing around in his mind. All he could do was sit and wait and hope for the best. He couldn't bear to think he might lose his Evelyn.

At last the door opened and Evelyn walked in. Bruno flung his arms around her and said, "I'm so glad to see you. I thought something had gone badly wrong. What happened? How is Jacob? Did Sarah catch you?"

"Stop, stop. Too many questions. Firstly let me get in then I'll tell you what happened."

There was no smile on her face that gave him a feeling that it was bad. He had shivers going up and down his spine.

………

Evelyn and Ingrid had met up at the place they had agreed on then made their way to Jacob. They didn't say much. There wasn't much too say. All they knew was they had to get to Jacob's as fast as possible. They were out of breath by the time they reached the small cul de sac that Ingrid had followed them to previously.

"It was half way down," said Ingrid, breaking the silence and speaking for the first time.

"Let's go down and try and judge where he might be."

"I don't want to get it wrong and knock on the wrong door. They might tell Sarah without realising the trouble they are causing."

Evelyn nodded in agreement.

"Well here we are half way down. Now to investigate to see if this is the one. Why don't we think of something quick and start knocking on doors?" questioned Ingrid.

That's what they did. In most cases it was the man answering the doors which they could understand as it was getting dark earlier now.

They came to one that stood out from the rest. Mostly the doors were uniform white but this one was red with what looked like a yellow star and a swastika painted on.

"This sounds typical of what I've heard about Sarah. Putting notices on their door is sending out a clear message," said Ingrid.

Evelyn just nodded. She was feeling very tense, wondering what they would find inside. Also she was worried in case Sarah came back and caught them at it.

"You looked worried," commented Ingrid. "It will be all right. You'll see."

Ingrid knocked on the door and they waited and they waited a bit more.

"I don't like this," whispered Evelyn.

"Neither do I but we're here now so we have to follow it through."

Evelyn nodded. "It's too quiet," she said.

Ingrid, ever the proactive, began looking around for any clues. She looked through a window and thought she saw something. Beckoning to Evelyn they both looked then turned to each other with grim faces.

"Do you think he's alive?" asked Evelyn.

"I don't know until I can get to him but he's certainly out of it."

"I know from what Bruno says that she used to drug him when she first got him home from hospital."

Ingrid looked grim. "That could be dangerous. She could easily give him too much. She has no training on the use of medication and could easily make a mistake. Or she could deliberately give him too much bring about his death."

Evelyn rapped hard on the window but no response. Jacob didn't stir.

"If you're looking for the lady who lives there you'll be in for a long wait. She went out earlier and she doesn't usually get back until late."

"We're actually looking for a man."

The man looked blank and shook his head. "Sorry I don't know anything about anyone else living there. It's just a young lady to my knowledge."

"Thank you for your time," said Ingrid who continued looking through the window. She desperately wanted the man to go back to his house so she could confer with Evelyn.

"I think we should come back another time," said Ingrid when on their own once again.

"But we'll probably find the situation the same as today."

"I wish we dare smash a window so something. I need to get in to make sure he's ok."

A slight movement caught Ingrid's eye and she looked through the window again. Sure enough, there was a slight stirring from the man in the bed they assumed to be Jacob.

Ingrid once again knocked. Jacob sat up and yawned. Gosh, he hadn't realised he was so tired. He felt a hangover affect which he assumed was sleeping so deeply through the afternoon. He heard the knock but when he tried to get off the bed he couldn't. In fact he couldn't even sit on the side of the bed. The handcuffs were used to keep his ankles tied to the bed but his arms were free. He tried manoeuvring his legs but couldn't. He needed the key which at a quick glance he didn't have. Doing strange sorts of actions he tried to indicate his plight to the two women he could see at the window.

"What's he trying to tell us?" asked Evelyn.

"I'm not sure, but he doesn't seem able to move his legs."

"Oh no, that wicked woman!" exclaimed Evelyn.

"You know what's wrong?" asked Ingrid.

Evelyn nodded, unable to respond immediately. Tears had come into her eyes and were running down her face. She turned away so Ingrid wouldn't see.

"It's ok," said Ingrid putting her arm around the other woman. "You need to tell me if we're to help Jacob."

"She's told Bruno that she keeps handcuffs attached to the bed. I know she hadn't used them up until now."

Ingrid gasped. She had realised that Jacob was in trouble but hadn't realised exactly how bad things were. She had hoped they would never get bad because she had been taking Bruno's advice, until then.

"What do we do?" asked Evelyn.

"I really don't know at the moment. We need a way to get into the house. Or we come again another day and hope she doesn't handcuff him."

"She usually keeps the house locked anyway."

"If it comes down to it we can smash the window but the downside would be that we would have to take Jacob there and then which might be too much for him."

"I don't think we can take too long before rescuing him. If she is handcuffing him things could escalate quickly. We don't know what else she might do to him."

Evelyn looked so despairing that Ingrid said, "Don't worry we'll sort something out."

"But how?"

"I don't know. I can only suggest we all get together and have another conflab about it. I'd rather we had a chance to get to know Jacob before taking him. We don't want to frighten him more than he already must be. We don't know what he thinks. He must be very confused as well. After all this is supposed to be his wife."

"Some wife she is."

"I know but he doesn't know that."

"Surely he could have worked it out for himself by now."

"Not necessarily. He is so used to being treated badly in the camps. We don't know what he may have witnessed or experienced himself."

Evelyn sighed.

Ingrid patted her arm saying, "Don't worry we'll sort something out quickly if we have to, but if we can, slowly until he starts to trust us."

Evelyn looked at her watch and said, "We better get going. The time is almost gone. We don't want Sarah coming back and finding us here."

"We certainly don't, that would be tricky and necessitate quick thinking and an urgent rescue plan."

They moved quickly away from the house after giving a quick wave to Jacob. They rushed away until they were some distance away and could avoid being caught by Sarah.

Evelyn with Ingrid soon reached the house. It had been decided without words that Ingrid would go back with Evelyn so they could talk with Bruno about the situation.

They found Bruno there before them. He was pacing up and down when they opened the door. He rushed through to them and took Evelyn in his arms. "I'm so glad you're home. I thought she might have caught you while you were there."

"We're fine," said Evelyn.

Bruno pulled away and acknowledged Ingrid with a smile which she didn't return.

"Something's happened hasn't it?"

The women could only nod as tears appeared in Evelyn's eyes.

"Oh no don't tell me we're too late," said Bruno, his heart hammering now.

"It's not that," said Ingrid seeing that Evelyn was unable to speak.

"Come on spit it out."

"It's just that he was dead to the world when we arrived. He didn't even stir when we knocked on the window. It was as if there was no one there at first. When he did wake up we discovered he was handcuffed to the bed by his ankles."

"No," said Bruno. "That bitch. She said she wasn't using them yet. I bet she's drugged him again as well. She's done that before.

I don't believe it she's given me the impression she's following my advice on dealing with Jacob."

"Drugged him? If that's the case we need to do something and fast. It could be a disaster other wise. She could easily overdose him either on purpose or by accident. Do you have any idea what she's using?"

Bruno shook his head. "Sorry I don't know. I don't think I could find out either. She would get suspicious if I suddenly started asking about it."

"No she wouldn't," said Evelyn for the first time. "You only have to say it's for me, that you need something to control me as I'm starting to get out of control and it's worrying you."

"You're a genius," said Ingrid, getting her hopes up. Maybe there was a way forward at least.

"You could always ask her to give you some. It might make it harder for her to drug Jacob if she gives away some of it. Once we know what it is I can look into it. That should tell us how urgent the situation actually is."

"I can do that in a couple of days when I see her. Will you be going to see Jacob again then?"

Evelyn turned to Ingrid for an answer. "I don't think it's worth it at the moment. We need to know what the exact situation is and work out our response before we do anything else."

Evelyn and Bruno agreed with that.

"Do you want a tea or coffee?" asked Bruno, suddenly remembering his manners.

"No it's fine thank you. I really must get going. But if you don't mind I'll come over in a couple of days after you've spoken to Sarah again."

Bruno nodded, "That's fine."

After Ingrid left, Bruno turned to Evelyn with a grim expression on his face. "It hadn't occurred to me she might take the drugging too far. I don't think we can wait too long."

Evelyn shook her head, "I really think we need Ingrid's help. She seems the more clued up one and maybe she's looking more objectively at the situation. It would take more than one of us to free him and if we went together we wouldn't know if Sarah's there or not. That would put all of us in jeopardy."

"I see your point. I wish I'd never got tied up with Sarah in the first place. I really don't see what I saw in her."

"If you hadn't we wouldn't have met. I don't regret anything as long as you are by my side."

"You're right of course. I don't regret meeting you. I do regret being brainwashed and joining the SS though."

"I don't blame you. Hitler was a charismatic personality and could talk anyone into believing anything he said."

"I know that now. He knew just what to say and he filled a gaping hole in my life."

"You've seen the error of your ways and realised he was so very wrong that's what matters now."

Bruno put his arms around Evelyn and held her tight, "I do love you, you know."

"And I love you too."

Ingrid was going over in her mind what she had witnessed that afternoon. How could Sarah treat Jacob like that. He hadn't done anything to deserve it, except for being born a Jew. She kept getting flashbacks of Jacob in handcuffs. Somehow she knew she would free him however hard the job was. She didn't care if she were killed in the trying as long as he were free to tell the authorities what he had been through and who Sarah really was.

Did Jacob even know who she was or did he still think she was his wife. She intended doing a search to see if she could find out what happened to the real Sarah. There had to be a record somewhere. She assumed she was in Auschwitz, at least to start with but what happened from there. The chances of survival were probably slim as she hadn't been looking for Jacob herself. The Red Cross would be the best place to start, they had records and she knew people were going to them for information about loved ones.

CHAPTER THIRTEEN

Ingrid was stood outside the Red Cross waiting for them to open. This had been the first opportunity she'd had to research the whereabouts of Sarah.

Finally in the building she found herself confronted with lists of names of those who had perished in what the Nazis had called The Final Solution. Was she really going to have to go through all those names, it was going to take for ever. She was glad she had come early and that it was her day off otherwise she wouldn't get her answers very quickly.

Approaching what looked like an official she began to ask her question only to be cut short with the comment, "You can see how busy we are and those list of names are up for a reason. If you can't find your loved one then see me again.

Ingrid sighed, there was no help for it she was going to have to read through the names. It wasn't going to be an easy job that was for sure. Oh well better get started, she thought. There was no time to waste and she had to meet Bruno and Evelyn that evening to discuss the next step. Bruno had seen Sarah a couple of days ago but because of her shift pattern she hadn't been able to come any earlier.

Scrolling through the names she wondered how she could identify the correct Sarah. It hadn't occurred to her she might need a surname so consumed was she in finding out the truth. She felt a bit silly as she left the building. There had been so many Sarah's. She hoped Bruno would know because she didn't think Sarah would give it away, at least not easily.

…………

They were sat around drinking coffee and talking generally before getting down to the business of Jacob. Bruno thought the surname was Stein but couldn't be certain. He knew it was a very Jewish sounding name. He hadn't registered it properly because it hadn't been relevant to the relationship he had with Sarah.

"I thought it would be good to give Jacob some information. It might help keep him going until we can get him away from there."

"It was a good idea," responded Bruno. "It hadn't occurred to us to find out but you're right, Jacob will want to know."

"What did you find out about the drug?"

"I didn't? Sarah was being very cagey when I asked her so I didn't pursue it further. I didn't want to make her suspicious. She wouldn't even say where she had got it from."

"Hmm….." said Ingrid, "This doesn't sound good at all. I hope it doesn't mean she suspected something."

"Surely not," said Evelyn.

"She's not stupid we know that. This is an ingenious plan she has and she's getting away with it. We have to hope somehow that she slips up at some point that will give us a way in."

"I wouldn't bet on it. She isn't stupid and she doesn't do slip ups. She is too ultra cautious. If I know her she's probably got bolts and keys to get into locked rooms."

Ingrid breathed a deep sigh and thought how skilful they would have to be. They hadn't give it any real thought until now.

"Look don't despair," said Bruno. "I'm sure we can get to the bottom of this."

"The problem is it seems so urgent," said Ingrid.

"I know but we can only take it one step at a time. If we rush things it will all go wrong and none of us will survive."

Ingrid looked sober as Bruno brought the reality of the situation home to her. It was serious and one wrong move and that would be it. They were dealing with a potentially volatile former SS officer who had killed and wouldn't hesitate to do so again.

Seeing Ingrid was lost for a response Bruno said, "Look I'll see if I can find out anything from Sarah. At least if we can get a surname we could find out about his wife. You two could go round there again while I'm with Sarah later today. At the very least it will let Jacob see you and know that someone knows of his existence. Hopefully he'll recognise you from last time."

"Sounds a good plan," said Evelyn speaking for the first time.

Ingrid just nodded. As much as she wanted to help Jacob she also had strong feelings of preservation and wasn't sure if it was a good idea to get involved further.

"You all right?" asked Evelyn.

Ingrid shrugged and said, "I'm not sure if it's a good idea to take this further. I guess I'm just realising the danger for all of us if this fails."

"We'd understand if you decided not to help, but we would really appreciate it if you would stay on board. I think it will take three of us to get this sorted," said Bruno.

Ingrid shook her head, "I'm sorry. I need time to think this through." She stood up and left the house without further word or look back

Bruno and Evelyn looked at each other. "Well it looks like it's just us," said Evelyn.

Bruno looked serious with his lips pursed together. "I'm not sure we can do it alone. I would need to have Sarah with me and you can't expect to get Jacob out and to safety alone."

"I hadn't thought of that. What can we do? We haven't got enough info to go to the authorities have we?"

"I think we can only hope that Ingrid will come back when she's had time to think. After all it was she who approached us not the other way around. She knew something was wrong so must have realised there could be some danger involved."

Evelyn nodded but said nothing.

"Look it's lunch time," said Bruno. "Why don't we go out for something to eat. We won't achieve anything just sitting here gloomily. It won't help Jacob."

Evelyn nodded and stood up going to get their coats.

They both were sat in the café they frequently went in. The waitress had said hello recognising them as regulars.

"Look who's just walked in," said Evelyn through a mouthful of cheese sandwich.

Bruno turned having his back to the door. He couldn't believe it. Ingrid. She looked surprised to see them but approached them nevertheless.

"I didn't expect to find you here," said Ingrid. "I came for lunch on my way to work."

"I thought it was your day off," replied Evelyn.

"It was but they called me in as they were short staffed."

Bruno nodded, unsure what to say. He decided to play it by ear and see what happened.

Seeing Bruno lost for words Evelyn said, "Why don't you join us?"

"Are you sure, I don't want to interrupt you."

"That's fine."

Ingrid pulled a chair over and sat on the end of the table. She indicated to the waitress that she wanted to order.

"It's on me," said Bruno. "So have what you like."

Ingrid hesitated, "Are you sure?"

"Absolutely certain."

"Thank you." Ingrid smiled for the first time since she'd sat down.

She was glad to have bumped into the couple as she had been doing some thinking and thought she may have been a bit hasty in leaving when she did. She remained quiet though, unsure what to say.

Deciding she might just as well say it straight out she said, "Sorry about earlier. It was wrong of me to walk out. There was no excuse."

"We understand," said Bruno. "You were feeling overwhelmed by the situation and needed some breathing space."

Ingrid nodded, "Thank you for your understanding. Now I've had time to think I still want to help if you want me to that is."

"Of course we want you," said Evelyn. "We're pleased you've changed your mind aren't we darling." Evelyn turned to Bruno who said nothing but turned and smiled at Ingrid.

"I obviously can't do anything tonight as I'm working but next time you see Sarah I hope I'll be able to be there."

"That will be in a couple of days," said Bruno, speaking at last.

"That's fine. I'm on early then so I can come by yours and we can plan our approach after my shift."

"Sounds good," said Evelyn, who was becoming enthusiastic again.

In her thoughts she had visions of a newly freed Jacob getting together and having a relationship with Ingrid. She didn't say this out loud as she didn't want to frighten Ingrid off and she knew Bruno would laugh and probably say something later when they were alone. It would be the ultimate perfect ending if it happened like that. This was real life though not a novel and things like that didn't usually happen outside of a book.

CHAPTER FOURTEEN

Evelyn and Ingrid were making their way to Jacob's. Sarah was safely with Bruno so they had time and of course this time they knew exactly where they were going so were faster. It wasn't long before they were knocking on Jacob's window. They knew better than to knock on the door this time and they knew which room was his. They were surprised to find Jacob sitting up with no handcuffs.

Bruno had obviously been chatting with Sarah last time about her attitude towards him again. He hadn't said anything but that was the only thing the two women could think of.

Jacob moved to the window and put his hands on the glass.

Ingrid put her hands up to reach out to his. They saw Jacob mouth the word help.

"We'll try," said Ingrid looking directly at Jacob hoping he would know what she said.

Jacob shook his head to indicate he hadn't understand. Ingrid repeated herself with a nod of her head at the same time. Jacob smiled, he had understood her this time.

The time soon passed, mostly with them standing there unsure how to communicate with each other to bring understanding.

It was Evelyn who eventually said, "We have to go now. We'll be back soon."

Ingrid indicated with her hand that they were leaving. Jacob's smile faded as he withdrew his hand realising the women were leaving.

"We'll be back soon," said Evelyn.

Jacob turned and went back to his bed and boredom. At least this time he had something to fill his thoughts.

………..

Jacob had achieved a partial understanding of his situation after he'd found himself in handcuffs. He didn't realise he was being drugged however. It was enough to know he was in danger and he knew without doubt anymore that this was not his wife Sarah. He didn't know her real name but knew enough to think she was pretending to be Sarah. It would explain why sometimes she didn't react if he called her by the name he knew her by.

He wondered what her real name was. He knew at least she was a German as she was fluent with no trace of an accent. He thought back to those days when he had first left hospital she seemed to dislike Jews with such intensity that made him believe she was a Nazi, probably a paid up member of the Party. His thoughts frightened him and he wondered how he could possibly escape when all doors and windows were locked. He knew this as he had checked. There was no escape and nothing had changed since he was beaten up. He had no longer had any trips out.

In his heart he knew she had probably set him up so that he would no longer talk about going outside again. She had been right, he was afraid at the thought. The problem was he needed to escape and that would mean going outside at some point.

Jacob had been so pleased to see the two women outside. It gave him hope to know that someone other than Sarah knew he was there. Had they realised his situation he had no way of knowing the answer to that. He could only hope. They were obviously there for him because they had stopped at his window and one of them had put her hands to match his on the other side. He longed for them to return and maybe they would get further. There must be a better way of communicating with them but didn't know what at that moment.

It was a situation he needed to keep from Sarah at all costs. His two new friends, as he thought of them, were coming when Sarah was out so they must know her routine. He was sure it was deliberate. These thoughts gave him hope and he realised it would help him cope with living with Sarah if he knew there were others who knew and would bring help if they couldn't help themselves.

He just hoped and prayed he wouldn't talk in his sleep and let the thing out of the bag. The problem was he wouldn't remember and Sarah wouldn't tell him that was certain. He had a tendency to talk in his sleep especially when disturbed by nightmares. He had been like that since a very young age and he knew it continued into adulthood as his real wife had told him and Sarah had mentioned something and used it as an excuse not to sleep with him anymore.

Jacob knew in his heart that the two women were going to be his rescuers. For that to happen he felt he would need to play his part. He had no keys to doors so would have to shout as loud as he could to be able to communicate better. He wanted to know what happened to his real wife Sarah as a matter of urgency. In his heart he suspected she had not survived the Nazi death camps. She hadn't been that strong and would never withstand half of what he went through. He knew that the women were treated in exactly the same way. The men were killed for flagging at all, so if they were, then surely the women would have done more so.

The key turning in the front door interrupted his thoughts. Sarah was back making his heart sink. In some ways he knew he was dependent on her but in others he was safer without her presence. He didn't know what would happen next.

"I'm home," said Sarah.

"Hello darling," Jacob said, hoping Sarah wouldn't know he had guessed at the truth of her identity.

"It's stew for dinner tonight. You can come and help prepare it if you want to."

Jacob jumped at the chance. It might give him a chance to see how things were. Maybe it would be a way of getting out of that place with the help of the two women at the window earlier.

Sarah and Jacob worked in silence with the occasional instruction from Sarah. As much as she'd like to starve him she knew she wouldn't get away with that, plus she needed him alive to keep her safe. If she were asked questions she could say she was married to a Jewish husband and she was a Jew. No one would suspect any different. All they had to do was ask Jacob to confirm her identity. She was still sure she had been clever enough for him not to work out who she really was.

As usual they ate their meal in silence. Sarah having nothing to say to a Jew and Jacob lost in his own thoughts. He had no wish to keep up the pretence any longer so he stayed quiet.

CHAPTER FIFTEEN

"I wish Ingrid were here then we could continue to work out our next move to free Jacob," said Evelyn.

"Am I not enough for you anymore?" asked Bruno.

"Of course you are my darling. I just don't like the idea of Jacob living what must be hell."

He is probably being treated better than he was in the camps."

"That's because of you. If it weren't she would be showing her true colours more than she is already. You are keeping him safe in a way because you do have some control over her."

"Not much, she's her own person. If anything it's the other way around."

Evelyn shook her head. "It used to be maybe but you have stood up to her and now it's the other way around. At least last time Jacob wasn't in handcuffs. I hate to think what the situation would be if it wasn't for you. I'm sure that woman has a screw loose."

"Maybe," said Bruno noncommittally.

Having finished eating Bruno and Evelyn cuddled up on the settee which they liked to do in the evening. They sat quietly together. So comfortable they didn't need to talk.

Evelyn sighed. It was one of contentment. Bruno looked into her face and kissed her firmly on the lips. "I do love you."

"I love you too," said Evelyn in return. "But I can't get my mind away from Jacob."

"I know, I'm the same but I'm sure we'll be able to do something soon. If only we could have a conversation with him."

"I've just had a thought."

"What is it? That we should go to bed and continue there."

"No. Silly," she thumped him playfully on the shoulder. "It's about Jacob."

"I might have known. I'm sure it's Jacob you're in love with instead of me."

"Now you are being silly. No I was thinking that next time we should take some paper with us with sentences on and hold it up for Jacob to read."

"Hey, you could be on to something there," said Bruno. "I hadn't thought of that. I bet Ingrid hasn't either. You're a genius." He looked down at his lover with pride. He'd landed himself a good one here and he wasn't about to let her go. He knew when he was on to a good thing.

Evelyn felt quite proud of herself. She'd never been called a genius before. It was rather a good idea she knew. She didn't want compliments though. What she wanted was to have a way of communicating with Jacob even if it was one way. At least it would be a way of letting him know they knew what was happening and were working on getting him out of there. It would at least give him some hope in the darkness, a ray of sunshine glimmering through the bleak situation.

…………

The three musketeers as they now referred to themselves were meeting again to discuss the next step of trying to rescue Jacob out of Sarah's clutches. Ingrid, when told of Evelyn's plan was very enthusiastic, especially as she hadn't come up with anything despite it constantly going around in her mind.

"I think we have to work out what to say and we'll need large writing just in case he's chained to the bed," said Ingrid.

"I think we need to keep it simple for this first time. Something like, we know your situation and hope to get you out soon. What do you think?" asked Evelyn.

"Hmm ok I suppose, but I think we could do better," said Bruno.

Ingrid was lost in thought, trying to come up with something simpler and more meaningful.

"We know and we care," suggested Evelyn before adding, "That was rubbish forget it."

"I can't come up with anything else," said Bruno. "We should go with Evelyn's first suggestion at least it gives hope."

"Agreed," said Ingrid. "I can't think of anything else either."

Bruno got a large piece of paper and started writing in large letters for Jacob to be able to see and read from a distance.

"I hope this works," said Evelyn, doubting herself now.

"It should do. It's an excellent idea and is better than just looking through the glass at him, unable to communicate, which achieves nothing except for him to know we are there. It must be so frustrating for him as well," said Ingrid.

"Right when do we do this?" asked Bruno.

"Next time you see Sarah I think. That's if it fits in with you and work Ingrid."

"It will be later today," said Bruno.

"That works well for me as I'm off today and then I have a week of late shifts so won't be able to do anything."

"I think we should tell Jacob that so he knows nothing will happen in the next week. As well it will let him know not to panic when he doesn't see us."

The other two agreed with Evelyn's suggestion and Bruno wrote it down on another piece of paper for them to show Jacob before they left him.

....

"I really think we should meet more often," said Sarah.

Bruno tried not to show the displeasure on his face. "I don't know if we can. We already meet three times a week," he protested.

"Don't you want to see me?" she asked somewhat petulantly.

"Of course I do it's just....."

"You want to see your other lover," said Sarah with some disdain in her voice.

"Don't talk like that. I didn't mean it to happen you know."

"How do I know that. For all I know you could have had secret love affairs with the Jews in the camps."

"Of course I didn't. How could you say such things. You know how I felt about them."

"Yes, I suppose, but you soon changed your tune when the war was over. Now look at you, you insist you are in love with scum."

"Don't talk like that about Evelyn. She's a lovely person." A lot better than you will ever be, he thought but didn't say aloud.

"If you say so. I don't know how you could. It's a pity we didn't get rid of more."

"Stop it, or I won't see you again," said Bruno, beginning to get angry now. He knew he shouldn't say that if they wanted to rescue Jacob but couldn't help himself.

"I could always turn you into the authorities and say you're torturing your lover because she's a Jew."

"Evelyn would soon vouch for me."

"Not if she's dead," said Sarah with a sneer.

"Are you threatening her?"

Sarah shrugged. "I think it's more of a promise."

Bruno really didn't like the way their conversation was going and felt helplessness and despair. Somehow he had to make Evelyn safe but he didn't know how not if they were going to continue trying to rescue Jacob.

"It's fine I'll meet you every night if that's what you want."

Sarah smiled, "It's all right. I knew you'd come round to my way of thinking soon."

Bruno felt terrible for letting Sarah manipulate him but didn't know what else to do. He was sure Sarah was wanting more of his time deliberately to keep him away from Evelyn. While Jacob was in danger though he had no choice just in case she carried out her threat and knowing her she would. He would be constantly looking over his shoulder.

....

Meanwhile, Evelyn and Ingrid were with Jacob, communicating through the window again. They held up the first piece of paper with the message on. Jacob stood at the window and read it. He nodded and smiled at the two women. He felt frustrated because he couldn't say anything back to them. He was encouraged though. It confirmed they knew what was happening and were working on it. He recognised Ingrid from the recent assault and knew she was a nurse.

During these brief window exchanges he could feel himself growing fond of Ingrid. She was a pretty young woman with brunette hair. She had laughter lines around her mouth which just added to the attraction as far as Jacob was concerned. Knowing his luck she was probably married with children. When she smiled her eyes sparkled. He told himself not to get attached to her, she probably wasn't interested anyway. After all who would want a Jew in their life as a romantic attachment.

Jacob tried speaking through the window but Ingrid shook her head to let him know they didn't understand what he was trying to say. How she wished she could lip read. It would be useful in her job as well.

Jacob found it frustrating that he couldn't speak back to them but was relieved from their note that they knew his circumstances and were working on getting him out of there. He felt hope rise inside of himself. He would get out of there at some point. He just wished it would be immediately, but realised it would take time and planning to do it. He wondered how they knew when Sarah was out but realised he probably wouldn't find the answer until the rescue came.

The time came for the women to leave Jacob. They held up the piece of paper to let him know they would be back. He smiled and nodded putting his thumbs up to let them know he understood.

After the women had left Jacob sat back on his bed with feet up relaxing. He hoped it wouldn't be long before he would be out of there and Sarah would be caught. He wondered why the women hadn't gone to the authorities with the information they had but thought they must have their reasons why they were doing it themselves.

....

Back at Bruno and Evelyn's the three of them went over what they had achieved.

"Jacob really seemed to appreciate our messages. He smiled and put thumbs up. I just wish we could get information from his side of things," said Ingrid.

"I feel the same as Ingrid," said Evelyn. "It's so frustrating and he looks as if he may have lost weight so I'm worried about what he maybe eating."

"I noticed that as well," said Ingrid.

"Is there any way you could pass a piece of paper and pen under the door for him to write something on?"

"I don't know, but it's a good thought," said Ingrid.

"Why don't we ask him when we're next there," suggested Evelyn smiling at Bruno whose idea it had been.

"Don't go all lovey dovey on me you two," said Ingrid.

"You're just jealous because you don't have anyone," said Evelyn.

"How do you know?"

"You wouldn't spend as much time helping us with this if you had, or you might have included him in helping you," replied Evelyn.

"You've got me there," said Ingrid.

"Look you two can we get back to business please or we'll be here until midnight," said Bruno.

The two women nodded.

"Ok what do you want me to write on the paper?"

"Just ask if he we can put paper and pen under the door for him to write on," said Evelyn.

Ingrid nodded her agreement.

"Did you get any information out of Sarah?" asked Evelyn when they'd taken care of messages for Jacob.

Bruno shook his head. "It was a disaster for us. Sarah wants to meet more often."

"Why's it a disaster? Surely it's a good thing as we can get more chances to visit Jacob and put a plan in place to rescue him," said Ingrid.

"I hadn't thought of it like that," said Bruno. "I was just thinking I'd be forced into her company and see less of Evelyn."

"That doesn't matter for now," said Evelyn. "It's only temporary. Once this is all over we'll have all the time in the world to be together."

"That's if we're all in one piece at the end of it," said Bruno grimly.

"Why do you speak like that?" asked Ingrid.

"Sarah is getting more threatening. I have no choice but to see her every night or she will take action."

"She could be bluffing," said Evelyn.

"She had a gun with her and pointed it at me."

"That doesn't mean much. After all it will be her loss if she kills you and she won't have so much protection either."

"I'm more worried she may get at you," said Bruno looking at Evelyn.

"She wouldn't dare. You would go straight to the authorities and that's her out of the way."

"True but I still don't trust her. I wish we could just get away from here somewhere she won't find us."

"What would happen to Jacob then. I can't do it on my own," pointed out Ingrid.

"I know," said Bruno. "He's the most important person in all of this. Unless we take what we know to the authorities now and leave it to them. Then we get away straight after that so if it goes wrong she won't find us."

"I don't trust them to sort it out properly. This country is in so much chaos with different countries overseeing it. There is a lot of rebuilding needed and a lot of dispossessed people turning up bit by bit having survived the Nazi camps throughout Europe."

"You're right there," said Bruno.

"So we're agreed with what we do next time then. If that's it I must get going. I'll see you in about a week when I'm next available in the evening."

Bruno and Evelyn stood up and went to the door to see Ingrid out.

Coming back in they went into each other's arms.

"I don't like exposing you to all this danger," said Bruno.

"It's fine and I want to help Jacob. It's my decision to carry on as we are."

"It's not safe and Sarah is becoming more volatile."

"I'm probably safer now than when I was in Bergen Belsen. If I'm not I certainly feel it here with you."

"Thank you," said Bruno leaning down to give her a long kiss.

When they pulled away Evelyn took him by the hand and led him upstairs to bed where they could really get down to business, in a pleasurable way.

"What are you looking so pleased about?" asked Sarah.

"Nothing in particular, just daydreaming really. I'm happy to have you back in my life. It's good to know we both survived that hell."

"I suppose so," said Sarah.

"You don't sound happy about it."

"Yes I am really," said Sarah still only half heartedly. She tried to smile at Jacob but couldn't quite manage it.

"Maybe you haven't properly adjusted to being free again," said Jacob.

"You could be right. I don't know," said Sarah.

"It is hard realising we are free at last especially after all we went through. The torture, the starvation, everything really."

Sarah just looked at him, feeling nothing. How could she reply without giving herself a way. She was at least relieved that he appeared not to realise she wasn't his beloved wife. She was sure she must have given herself away loads of times. He must be really stupid, she thought, not to have got the message yet. Typical Jew really.

"Anyway I'm tired so I'm off to bed," said Jacob.

On his way to his room he turned and said, "Why don't you come with me we can cuddle up together like we used to."

Sarah shuddered at the thought, then smiled and said, "I'd prefer to sleep alone. I don't want to disturb you with my nightmares," she lied.

"You won't. I have them as well so we can reassure each other and know we are safe now."

Sarah just shook her head and turned away to let Jacob know the conversation was over. She couldn't see herself sleeping in the same bed as Jacob anymore. It was bad enough when she did.

Jacob laid awake looking up at the ceiling with arms under his head. He looked more relaxed than he felt. He was desperately trying to keep up the pretence that he believed Sarah to be his wife but it was so hard. He hated this woman with a passion, knowing who she was. He longed to get out and see her locked up so she couldn't prey on anymore vulnerable people. The one thing keeping him going was the visits from the two women. He didn't know who they were but they seemed to be on his side and knew he was being kept as a prisoner. At least he had a nice comfortable bed and wasn't made to sleep on those hard bunks they had in the camp.

He longed to know what had happened to the real Sarah but assumed she must be dead as she hadn't turned up yet, unless she was searching for him. He needed to be free so he could find out what happened to her. He was prepared for the worst but hoped still for a miracle. They did happen occasionally.

CHAPTER SIXTEEN

"I've got a really bad feeling about this," said Evelyn to Ingrid as they made their way to Jacob's.

"Are you sure it's not just the situation making you feel like that?"

"I don't think so. It just feels as if we are putting ourselves in danger today."

"We are every time we come."

"I know but this feels different somehow. I can't explain it properly."

"You think Sarah is going to come back early and catch us?"

"Maybe I'm really not sure. It's a feeling inside that's all."

Ingrid gave up on the questioning and they continued on in silence.

They found Jacob at the window. He seemed agitated and was desperately signing something to them. They weren't sure what he was getting at. He kept looking towards the bedroom door.

Evelyn felt a strong sense of unease as they stood there trying to work out what he was communicating. Ingrid started to speak but Evelyn put her finger to her lips to silence her.

It was at that moment the bedroom door opened and Sarah walked in.

Ingrid gasped, she hadn't expected that. She wished she had listened more to Evelyn now but really had taken no notice, sure it was nothing.

Evelyn, already on the alert ducked down low and pulled Ingrid with her so they wouldn't be seen.

"What are you doing at the window?" asked Sarah looking out but seeing nothing.

"I just wanted to see the world that's all."

"See the world," said Sarah scornfully. "There's only a brick wall out there. What rubbish are you talking now."

"It's still better than seeing barbed wire everywhere with guards in towers with guns trained on us ready to shoot."

"I suppose you're right," said Sarah, realising she better be careful what she said or she'd say something she would later regret. She was still certain Jacob didn't know her true identity and she intended it to stay like that.

Sarah followed his gaze and tried to see what he saw in a brick wall. She moved closer to the window and Jacob held his breath not wanting her to look down and see the two women Jacob now saw as his friends.

"We need to get out of here," whispered Ingrid wishing she had listened to Evelyn's worries instead of dismissing them. Now here they were in danger if Sarah were to notice them.

Evelyn nodded but didn't say a word. Very slowly they crept away not standing until they reached the end of the alley and had turned the corner. They dared to stop to catch their breath, both of them realising they had been holding it, such was the terror they felt at nearly being caught.

"Phew that was a close one," said Evelyn, still leaning over, hands on her knees struggling to breathe.

"It's ok," said Ingrid. "Take some slow deep breaths, that's right."

Gradually Evelyn's breathing settled down and she stood up. "That was scary."

"What was? Nearly being caught or your rapid, shallow breaths?"

"Both I think."

Ingrid nodded and said, "If you think you can move now we should leave this area before Sarah decides to investigate further."

"Why would she?"

"We don't know what Jacob said or if she worked out there was someone out there."

"I see your point."

The two women hurried away. Every now and again they looked behind them but neither saw nor heard anyone. No rustling in the bushes nor sight of a human. They kept going, not daring to stop just in case…

They soon reached Evelyn's house where Bruno had the door open before they'd even reached it.

The relief on his face was palpable. "I'm so pleased to see you," he said. "I've been so worried. Sarah didn't turn up and I thought she might catch you."

"It was a close call," said Ingrid, "But we managed to duck down quick and make our escape. I don't think she realised anyone was there but we didn't dare stop until now."

"Thank God!"

Bruno took Evelyn into his arms and held her tight. He could feel her heart going rapidly and the rigidity of her body. Although she hadn't said anything he felt her fear that was still there.

"Come in, the pair of you and we can talk," said Bruno. Looking down at Evelyn he continued, "It's all right you're safe now."

Sitting on the settee they tried to relax. Bruno made them a hot cup of tea, which they sipped slowly. Evelyn's hands were still shaking which Bruno and Ingrid noticed with some concern.

"Are you all right?" asked Bruno of Evelyn.

She shook her head. "I can't get away from how close we were to being caught. I was so scared. It's brought back to me how we were treated, just getting through the day waiting for death."

"I'm so sorry. I had no idea of what it must have been like for you. I feel so guilty that I was part of the system that did that to you and millions of others."

"You don't need to feel guilty, you're a good man."

"But I was there as an SS officer, I took part in the systematic abuse and killings of Jews and other minorities."

"But you're not like them."

"I was. There is no getting away from the fact that at the time I believed in what we were doing."

"You've seen the error of your ways and have changed so much."

"That's down to you my darling. Really I should hand myself in and take whatever punishment is due to me."

"Don't do that. I need and love you too much."

"I should go," broke in Ingrid at this point. She felt uncomfortable listening to the intimate conversation between the two of them. They seemed to have forgotten she was there.

"No don't go. We need to talk about what went wrong today and try and avoid it happening again."

"Did you know Sarah wasn't going to turn up?" asked Ingrid.

Bruno shook his head. "I waited in the usual place but she didn't come. I became concerned for the pair of you, but also for Jacob in case Sarah had been captured."

"She was definitely at home and fine. We can vouch for that."

"So we still have no idea why she stayed at home."

"You…you don't think maybe she guessed something was wrong and stayed at home hoping to catch us do you."

"I don't think that's the case," said Bruno. "I've certainly never said anything."

"Are you sure she didn't pick up on anything from your body language."

"I would hope not as I'm always very guarded with her."

"Maybe that's the problem she sensed it within you and became suspicious."

"I doubt it," said Bruno looking at Ingrid and seeing suspicion in her face. "You don't believe me do you."

"I have my doubts," said Ingrid with brutal honesty. "After all you have already reminded us you were a member of the SS as was Sarah so you might still have some loyalty there."

"But I'm in love with Evelyn. You don't think that could happen if I were still believing that nonsense do you? I thought you knew me better than that."

"I don't know, I really don't."

"Evelyn what do you think?" asked Bruno turning back to his lover.

"I believe you. The love I've felt from you is genuine."

Bruno smiled tenderly at her. Ingrid could see the love in his eyes and said, "I could have made a big mistake. I'm sorry to suspect you."

"No, you don't have anything to apologise for. I deserve your doubts after all I did."

"I wasn't taking in the fact that you have changed and I can see that now when I see the love you show for Evelyn. You wouldn't do anything that would hurt her in any way."

"Thank you. I do appreciate it as I still carry that guilt around with me."

"Let it go. Evelyn has forgiven you now you have to forgive yourself. You were following orders, doing your job. If you had refused you would have found yourself in dire circumstances or maybe even dead."

"I agree," said Evelyn.

"Thank you both of you. I appreciate it."

"I think I had better be going and leave you to it."

"You don't have to."

"Yes I do. It's for the best. I'll come back tomorrow and we can discuss what we do from here to be sure of the safety of all of us."

Bruno nodded.

With Ingrid gone the couple continued to kiss and enjoy being with each other.

"Are you sure you're all right?" asked Bruno, sensing a reluctance in Evelyn.

"Yes I'm fine. It's just everything. I was so scared and thought I would never see you again and you wouldn't know what had happened."

"I understand, I really do. I would be the same in your situation especially as we know Sarah is dangerous."

CHAPTER SEVENTEEN

"Where were you yesterday?" asked Bruno bluntly.

"I was testing," responded Sarah.

"What?"

"I thought maybe you had told someone and they were visiting Jacob when I wasn't there."

"That's silly."

"Is it? I'm not so sure. You've been distant with me lately and getting close to that Jew of yours. You know the situation with Jacob and might want to help get him away from me."

"So what? You expected me to rescue him?"

"You see when you talk like that you can't blame me for being suspicious."

"How can I do anything when I'm with you?"

Sarah was stuck for words.

"You can't answer that can you. Don't you see how ludicrous you sound?"

Sarah nodded. "You could be right," she said, not wanting to admit that she sounded stupid.

"I know I'm right. Now come here I've missed you," said Bruno drawing Sarah to him and kissing her.

"Mm that's better," murmured Sarah.

Bruno felt like a traitor to Evelyn but felt he needed to make Sarah believe she was wrong in her assumptions. The reality was he had grown to hate Sarah and wished he'd never started a relationship with her in the first place. In his eyes she was now pure evil.

Bruno really hated himself. The sooner they got Jacob out of there and to safety the sooner he could get away from Sarah by giving himself up if he had to. He knew he would receive no mercy from the authorities. They wouldn't care how much he'd changed they would look only at the war crimes he'd committed and he could possibly be facing the severest punishment – death.

He really needed to prepare Evelyn for this. She needed to know the worst case scenario. Obviously he hoped he could just slip away somewhere quietly just the two of them but that might not be the best way forward. That way he would always be looking over his shoulder sure he was about to be caught, forever on the run. Sarah, he was sure, would implicate him as soon as she was arrested to try and do a deal.

He made up his mind to speak to Evelyn that night as soon as she got home from Jacob's.

....

Ingrid and Evelyn were finally having a real conversation with Jacob. Passing the paper under the door with a pen had worked and he was able to write messages to the two women.

"Thank you for wanting to help me," he said.

"We will get you out of there," said Ingrid. "I promise you it will be as soon as we can but we have to take it slowly and make careful plans. We already think Sarah has become suspicious."

Jacob shrugged, not knowing anything and having nothing to say in response. He put his hand to the glass of the window and Ingrid put hers against his.

Ingrid couldn't say what it was but something was stirring inside her. She really admired Jacob who had been through so much and now when he should be safe and learning to live again he was trapped, kept a prisoner by a former SS guard who was a sadist. There was no other way of describing Sarah who was still living in the past. Ingrid felt she should probably feel sorry for Sarah but she didn't. She hated her for what she was doing to this man who had already been through so much.

Evelyn looked at the pair and had her own thoughts. What would be more perfect than the two getting together when Jacob was properly free. Maybe a little matchmaking was called for. She would speak to Bruno about it.

Meanwhile Ingrid had no idea that Evelyn had read her so accurately.

"Instead of eyeing each other up maybe we should say something else and get more information from Jacob?" Evelyn suggested.

Ingrid blushed and removed her hand. She wrote on a piece of paper asking Jacob what Sarah was doing with him to try and gauge how urgent the situation was.

Jacob immediately began writing furiously on the paper desperate to portray an accurate description of his life, including the sleeping he did, the handcuffs, locked doors and windows, little food were just some examples of the ways he was being treated.

Ingrid turned away not wanting Jacob to see the tears well up on hearing this although it was what they already guessed and what Bruno had told them. Evelyn saw the tears and thought all the more that the two of them were meant for each other. She would definitely sus out the situation and try and push them together.

Ingrid asked Evelyn, "Do you think we should tell him about being drugged?"

"I don't know. It might take away his concerns about the tiredness he is suffering from but might cause further anxiety which he might not be able to keep hidden from Sarah then the situation could become critical."

Ingrid nodded her agreement.

"We probably should go," said Evelyn, "Or we might find ourselves getting caught and that's the last thing we want. It nearly happened the other night and I don't want that again thank you very much."

"I agree," said a reluctant Ingrid.

Evelyn quickly wrote a note for Jacob telling him they'd be back soon and hopefully have more information by then.

The two women hurried away. Suddenly Evelyn stopped and pulled Ingrid into a bush to hide.

"I thought I saw Sarah in the distance walking in our direction."

Ingrid peered out slightly and pulled her head straight back in nodding at Evelyn.

They stayed where they were, hearing footsteps getting closer. The two women held their breaths, not wanting to make even the slightest noise that would alert Sarah to their presence. They watched Sarah pause and look behind her then shook her head and continued walking passed where Ingrid and Evelyn were. They let her get well away from them before coming out of hiding.

"Phew that was close," muttered Ingrid. "I really thought she had us for sure."

"So did I," said Evelyn.

"Come on let's move away. I won't feel safe until we get back to your place."

The women moved on at a jog until they ran out of energy and slowed down to a brisk walk.

Bruno was looking out for them and opened the door, "What is it?" he asked with some concern. "You both look flushed as if you've been running."

Ingrid explained what had happened.

"I did wonder but I'm just glad you got back here and that there was a convenient bush for you to hide behind."

"It was probably our fault," said Evelyn, "We were probably a bit late leaving Jacob." She cast a meaningful glance at Ingrid which Bruno didn't understand but he knew he would find out later what was going on.

"We do have a slight problem though. Sarah is saying she can't bear to be with Jacob much longer."

"Does this mean she'll take action?" asked Ingrid concerned. She flushed but only Evelyn guessed why.

"I really don't know," said Bruno running his hands through his hair. "I'm so stressed I don't know what to do."

"We have to do something. Maybe we need to act faster than we thought. What exactly did she say?" asked Evelyn.

Ingrid was lost for words. Her heart started pounding in her chest. She was sure the other two could see and hear it just as loudly as she could in her ears.

"She said she couldn't bear to live with Jacob any longer. She felt he was putting pressure on her to sleep together again. Living with a Jew was disgusting and made her feel as if she had to scrub herself clean."

"Not good," said Evelyn. "What should we do? Why can't we just go to the authorities with what we know and let them take it from there. To protect Jacob we could always get them to come to her when she next meets you. That should protect Jacob and prevent any backlash if she got to her gun first."

"I'm not sure that's such a good idea," said Ingrid. "What if it backfires and the authorities either don't believe us or arrest Bruno as well."

"I don't think we can avoid that," said Bruno. "In fact if we decide to take this approach I should give myself up and hope for the best."

"I can't bear to lose you," said Evelyn tears pricking her eyes.

"I know my darling, but I think it's the only way. At least if I give myself up voluntarily they might go easy on me."

"I'll speak up for you as well. They'll see what I feel for you and after all I've been through they'll see that and accept it."

"We have to face facts though. It may not happen," said Ingrid.

"That's true," said Bruno. "They may only look at what I've done and want to try me as a war criminal."

"But you've changed."

"That won't make any difference to them they'll just see what I've done. I may get the severest punishment. At the very least I'll probably get a jail sentence for a long time."

Evelyn burst into tears, unable to bear listening to what was being said whilst acknowledging the truth in what her lover was saying. Bruno put his arms around her and held her tight. She clung to him for dear life unwilling to let him go but knowing she must be prepared to say good bye to him forever.

Ingrid's heart was heavy. She had no words to comfort the pair. She knew the truth had already been spoken. This would not end well she was sure of it. Hitler and his evil was still continuing even after his death and the armies that had taken over were determined to get all the war criminals and punish them for what they had done.

Bruno pushed Evelyn back gently before saying, "When do we do this? We'll have to persuade them I'm not a danger so I can be at the meeting place for Sarah."

"As soon as possible," said Ingrid. "We can't leave Jacob there in that toxic, volatile situation. Who knows what Sarah may do next."

Bruno nodded his agreement. "I've agreed to see her again tomorrow so I suggest we go now if we all agree."

"No," said Evelyn, "Let me at least have one last night with you."

Bruno begun, "No……We haven't time to waste, we need to get on with it for Jacob's sake."

Ingrid said, "I'm sure another night won't hurt. We will go in the morning. I'll be here first thing and the three of us will go together."

Bruno nodded his agreement with that plan. It was a relief to have one more night with his darling Evelyn.

"Why don't you stay the night with us to save you leaving and coming back?" suggested Bruno.

Much to Evelyn's relief Ingrid shook her head, "No, I should leave and let you two lovebirds have some time alone together. After all you don't know when you'll get another chance."

Picking up her things Ingrid moved to the door and let herself out.

Bruno and Evelyn sat on the sofa in each other's arms.

Bruno asked, "So what is going on then. I sensed something when we were talking about Jacob and his situation. It was Ingrid."

"I think she is developing feelings for him."

"Really! That would be great."

Evelyn nodded, feeling sad. She agreed it would be good for Jacob and Ingrid. Jacob deserved something good to happen in his life and she couldn't think of a nicer person than Ingrid. She would be understanding if he still had nightmares or needed to talk.

"Hey it's going to be all right," said Bruno.

"How can you be so sure?"

"It's just this feeling I've got. It should help that I'm giving myself up as well as in a relationship with you."

"Maybe. My concern is that Sarah will do her best to sabotage you."

"She probably will but I'll take my chances."

"Couldn't we just leave."

Bruno shook his head, "That's not the right thing to do. It won't be safe for Jacob, in fact it would be a disaster for him. We would also be forever looking over our shoulders just in case...."

"You're probably right."

"I know I am. If I were to get caught later it would be worse for me."

"Let's just go to bed."

Bruno gave a wicked smile and said, "I agree. An early night should definitely be on our agenda."

They lay together in each others arms not saying anything. They had just enjoyed themselves and now were relaxing together, half dozing. Evelyn was doing her best to stay awake, wanting to savour every last moment with Bruno that she could.

Bruno began kissing her again. He knew this would be the end although he was keeping that to himself. He believed strongly that he would never see Evelyn once he'd given himself up. He had done some wicked things in Hitler's name that he was now ashamed of. He was willing to be open and honest when he gave himself up to try and assuage the guilt he now lived with. He knew what he had done was wrong and the way he felt was eating him up inside. It would in fact be a relief to actually put his hands up and admit to everything. He felt that the only way he could be at peace with himself would be if he was hung for what he had done.

Evelyn lay stiff, unable to relax. Like Bruno, she had the sense that this was for the last time. It more than saddened her. She knew if she were to lose him she would never sleep with another man again. She wouldn't be able to, she would always see Bruno in her mind. She would never love again and it made her sad.

Neither of them slept much that night, although they spent most of the time in silence. There were no words that either felt able to express. They both hated to say good bye and felt if they didn't maybe they would have the chance to be together again even if it wasn't straight away.

....

Ingrid, too, had a sleepless night. She was worried about her three friends. It would be so sad if Evelyn was going to have to suffer losing Bruno. She had already been through too much and lost everything and nearly her life. She didn't know how things would go for Jacob but hoped it would all work out and that he would be able to forge a new life for himself. She would like to think it would include her as an intimate relationship but couldn't guarantee that. It would depend if he could ever get over losing his real wife and possibly never know exactly what happened to her. She still had some investigating to do but maybe get Jacob out of there and he could help her with the search. It might help him feel useful and accept the reality of his situation. She would make sure she was there for him no matter what. She would settle for friendship if that was all he was able to offer.

The war had so many casualties, especially in the Nazi occupied countries. People disappearing in the middle of the night never to be seen again. What a tragedy had befallen them. She didn't have faith in God but if she had she would have lost it over all the suffering. How could a God, any God allow it to happen and not step in sooner especially to His so called chosen people. That was what the Jews insisted they were.

Ingrid gave a huge sigh as if she had the burdens of the world on her shoulders, which was the way she felt at that moment. Life was too hard and for some unbearable.

Jacob, too, was awake. Sarah really was sadistic he thought. He had been made to stand in the corner of her bedroom and told he must spend the night like that. He was not allowed any sleep, neither could he sit down. It was becoming difficult. All he wanted to do was sleep. He didn't know how Sarah could sleep at night after all she had done not just to him now but to those in the camps. She seemed to be having a peaceful sleep. He wondered if he could get away with sitting on the floor. At least if sitting he might be able to doze off, but then what would happen if she were to wake before him? The thought didn't bear thinking about. He wasn't sure he wanted to find out either, even though he was dead on his feet.

"Get me a cup of tea slave," barked Sarah the next morning.

"What do you mean slave. I'm not your slave, I'm your husband."

"Husband, don't even call yourself that."

"Why are you speaking like that darling?"

"Don't call me darling. I'm not your darling. Haven't you worked out that yet? You must be more stupid than I thought."

"Who are you?"

"I was an SS officer in the women's camp at Auschwitz Birkenau."

Jacob didn't gasp already having worked most of this out for himself long ago but had to keep up the pretence for his own safety.

"The war is over the Nazi party is dead. You would be much happier if you accepted that and recognised that what you did was very wrong."

"I did what I was ordered to and proud of it. Hitler offered us a much better life but in the end he proved himself a coward and took the easy way out. Well I'm not like that. I'm a survivor and a fighter. I will get through this, although it may not be with a filthy Jew."

"Why did you pretend to be my wife? I don't understand."

"None of your business."

"But it is when it's my life you're messing with."

"Life? What life? You're not entitled to a life. You're Jewish."

There was such scorn on her face that Jacob had never seen before. She really believed what she was saying. He almost felt sorry for her, that she could be so full of hatred. She was missing out on so much.

He shook his head. "You know I feel sorry for you."

"Well don't. I'm quite happy with my life except for having to put up with you."

"Leave then."

"Me leave. It's my flat if anyone leaves it'll be you. But what makes you think I would let you out of here alive."

Sarah picked up her gun and pointed it at him.

"There isn't any need for that. With all the doors locked I can't get out of here. If you shoot me all the neighbours will hear and call the police."

"I think not. They're all criminals themselves. I'll soon get them out of here then shoot you. No one will be any the wiser. No one knows you're here."

Jacob opened his mouth then shut it again. He nearly gave his new friends away and admitted they existed. Fortunately he thought better of it. He knew Sarah wouldn't hesitate to use that gun on his friends. He didn't want them in trouble for helping him.

Next time they came he would have to get a message to them to let them know Sarah had finally given herself away and was treating him really badly. As far as he could tell she was escalating into further violence and he was no longer safe with her.

CHAPTER EIGHTEEN

Bruno was getting ready to go to the authorities. His hands were shaking and there were purple bruises under his eyes which told of a sleepless night. He had kept up the bravado in front of Evelyn and Ingrid but inside he was a nervous wreck. He really wished there was another way out of it but this was all they could come up with that was sensible. He didn't want to spend the rest of his life hiding, he had to face up to the reality of what he'd done and now the consequences.

There was a knock at the door which Evelyn got. It was only Ingrid who was going to support the couple and be there for Evelyn if the worst should happen and Bruno was locked up.

"You look terrible," remarked Ingrid.

"I don't look as bad as I feel. You should see Bruno. Neither of us slept much last night if at all."

"I'm sorry to hear that but we have to stay positive and focused. This will work out all right," said Ingrid sounding more reassuring than she felt.

She wasn't at all sure it would go the way they wanted it to. They really were being tough on the Nazis who had committed war crimes. Yes, Bruno had changed and was full of remorse but there was no hiding the fact that he had been based in the death camps and therefore would be seen as a war criminal for committing crimes against humanity.

Ingrid looked up and saw Bruno walking down the stairs. Evelyn hadn't been wrong he really did look terrible, as if he hadn't slept in a year.

"Come on then, let's get this over with," said Bruno, trying to sound cheerful but not fooling anyone.

He took a deep breath and stepped outside. They had decided to walk to their destination as Bruno wanted to savour the luxury of fresh air that he might be denied of for a very long time and possibly forever. They made their way in silence, Bruno stopping every few minutes to sniff the air that was full of the scent of flowers. It was amazing that the flowers had survived to give hope to the people where everything else was in ruins from the bombs that had been dropped months before the end of the war. Everywhere was grey rubble. People walked by, heads down, in a hurry not wanting to look around at the devastation that existed all around them.

Every now and again they would pass a soldier in British or American uniform. It served as a reminder of what had happened in their country. The people still could not think about how they could go about rebuilding Germany. They were beaten and they knew it. Hitler hadn't been the saviour they had thought him. He had unleashed a reign of terror and many people still walked around in fear. No one knew when the Gestapo may approach and forcibly take them. They had lived like that for too long and many couldn't believe it was now over, they were free.

Bruno and the two women eventually reached the building they were heading towards. There were lots of soldiers going in and out all the time. Bruno stopped before going up the steps and looked around one last time. Taking a deep breath he walked up the steps flanked by the two women who had no intention of leaving his side unless absolutely necessary.

"Can I help you?" asked the security man at the door.

"We have information about a former SS officer," said Ingrid, seeing the other two lost for words.

"Ok, when you enter turn left and go up to the desk."

"Thank you," said Ingrid with a smile.

On entering they looked around them at the high ceiling and the big space. There were tables in different directions with women sat behind them in uniform. Bruno and the women went to the desk on the left as directed. Again it was left to Ingrid to tell the lady at the desk what they were there for.

The lady picked up the phone and said something in English which neither of the three could understand.

"Someone will be with you shortly," said the lady in German.

"Thank you," said Ingrid.

The trio moved slightly to the side and waited. They saw grim faced men walking down the stairs on the far side of the massive lobby area and approach them.

"Are you here about the SS officer who is currently in hiding?"

Bruno nodded.

"If you'd like to come with us."

They followed the men through a maze of passageways with rooms going off in different directions.

"I'd get lost in here," commented Ingrid.

"You'd soon get used to it," said one of the officers. "Ok here we are. After you," he said, holding the door open for the trio to enter first.

They sat down in silence and the officers introduced themselves as Major Trott and Sergeant Lamb.

Major Trott took the lead while his sergeant opened a notebook and picked up his pen ready to write any information down.

Bruno decided he really was going to have to give the information as he knew a lot more than the women.

He finished the sorry tale and looked up at the grim faces of the officers before them.

"How do we know you're telling the truth. We have so many people in claiming to know a war criminal only to find out it's a load of lies and just someone having a grudge against the accused."

"I'm telling the truth because I was there. I witnessed it as I too, was an SS officer based mostly in Auschwitz Birkenau. I am not proud of it. I see know how wrong I was but Hitler could be so persuasive that we just went along with everything without questioning it. I now have a girlfriend, Evelyn, a Jew who was a survivor of one of the camps."

"So you're telling us you were involved as well?" queried Major Trott.

Bruno nodded. "I got involved with Sarah and we had a relationship which she would like to think is still going. She has been forcing me to continue to see her on a regular basis and she tells me how she is treating Jacob. She has recently become fed up of living with him so the three of us feel he is in more danger than previously."

"Why didn't you come to us earlier with this? It looks a bit suspicious to me. How can we be sure it's true?"

"You only need to go with the women here who can take you to where they are living. You will see Jacob there."

"If you're right surely us turning up will put Jacob in more danger."

"We know that which is why we are suggesting you go when Sarah meets up with me tonight. There will be no one except Jacob in the flat. Evelyn and Ingrid have been going regularly and exchanged messages with him."

Major Trott nodded and looked at his sergeant who also nodded.

"Ok we can do that. We will have to ask you more questions about your role though sir."

"I understand that."

"Can we stay with him?" asked Evelyn.

"I'm afraid not. You can wait though and we'll let you know what's happening."

"If you're questioning him how can he be at the meeting place to meet Sarah?" asked Ingrid.

"That's a good point," said Sergeant Lamb.

"We'll let you go for now and see what happens tonight. I'm putting you on your honour that you won't try and disappear in the meantime either with these two women or with Sarah."

"I won't."

Major Trott nodded and shook hands with the three on the way out, having agreed to be near the meeting place to intercept Sarah and Bruno. Actually he could see it would make sense doing it that way because then Sarah wouldn't realise who it was who had said something. All he had to do now was get a team ready. He, himself, was going to capture the two SS officers and leave a couple of officers to meet Ingrid and Evelyn in the park and go to rescue Jacob.

"Phew I'm glad that's over," said Bruno.

"Not yet it's not," pointed out Evelyn.

"The worst part is."

"Not really. They still want to question you and we don't know what they'll say."

"I understand what you're saying but in my mind the worst is over. Actually telling them the situation with Sarah and admitting my involvement was the hardest. They know now so it's in their hands. All I've done is tell the truth. They can ask any questions needed to compile any reports as necessary. It's a relief not having to hide anymore. It's out in the open for them to do with me as they see fit."

"I agree with you now you put it so clearly," said Ingrid.

She turned to Evelyn and saw the tears sliding quietly down her face. "Hey, it's going to be all right, you'll see. They'll see what a good man Bruno is really and let him go."

"You don't know that for sure," said Evelyn sniffing back the tears.

Ingrid had nothing to answer with. No, she knew there was some doubt in her mind as well, but she felt Evelyn needed some positive thinking here to keep her going. It was going to be a difficult few hours or days and there was no telling how it would end up. As well as being there for Bruno and Evelyn she was also thinking of Jacob and getting him out of that toxic environment. Her main concern was that it would all go according to plan with Sarah and Jacob. There was always an element of doubt there ever since Sarah hadn't turned up once before. In her mind it made Ingrid think it could happen again and that Sarah was suspicious of something.

CHAPTER NINETEEN

Bruno stood in the usual place by the pond. Behind that there was a small shack that was empty all year around. Sarah liked them to go in there as it was unlikely they wouldn't be disturbed. This time, however, it was being used by Major Trott and his team. They were keeping out of the way, while they waited for Sarah to turn up.

Bruno was pacing back and forth, anxiety eating away at him. What if she didn't turn up that would lead everything into a difficult position and put everyone in danger back at the flat. Also it would badly reflect on him if she didn't turn up. It may look as if he made it up on purpose to avert them to the real danger – him!

Bruno breathed a huge sigh of relief when she came striding across the grass towards him. He moved round the pond and approached her.

The soldiers in the shack were watching and waiting for the right moment. Bruno would take her in his arms and start leading her towards the shack. Before they got there the watchers burst out and surrounded the couple. They told them their rights and arrested them immediately.

"You're coming back to headquarters with me," said Major Trott.

"Who are you?" asked Sarah. "I can assure you we are both above board. I'm a Jew although this man is a fully paid up member of the Nazi party."

Bruno gasped, "If that were true why would I be standing here talking to this Jew."

"You will both need to come back and I will need to see your credentials."

Sarah not being prepared said, "I don't have anything on me."

"That's all right it's not necessary because I can still prove who you are."

Sarah paled, it sounded as if they knew what they were doing. How could they have found her. No one knew who she really was she was certain. She would be suspicious of Bruno but surely he wasn't stupid enough to hand himself in.

He was resistant to being arrested so struggled as they put handcuffs of to make it more genuine for Sarah's benefit.

………

Meanwhile, Ingrid and Evelyn had made their way to the flat where Jacob and Sarah lived. The authorities were accompanying them to help get Jacob out and at provide some protection against Sarah or anyone else should it be needed.

They reached the flat and Ingrid immediately went to the window. To her horror Jacob wasn't in his room as usual. He was expecting them so something must be wrong. Ingrid and Evelyn were instantly on their guard. The officers realising the problem offered to look around and see what they could find. So the officers led the women around to other windows. No one could see any signs of life which would indicate Jacob's presence and wellbeing.

"I don't think we can put any message through the door either because it might be seen by Sarah," said Evelyn.

"But Jacob maybe in trouble. We can't just leave him," said Ingrid.

"We have no choice but to leave it for today. She has obviously done something."

The officers looked at each other wondering if this was genuine or staged in some way.

"We'll come back tomorrow. I wonder if anyone is letting her know of our presence here."

"How can that be?" asked Ingrid. "No one knows."

"How can we be sure?" asked Evelyn. "We don't really know anything about the neighbours. All we know is they probably don't know about Jacob."

"Here come the officers. Let's see what they have to say."

"The place seems completely empty. How many bedrooms are there do you know?"

"At least two," said Ingrid.

"Hmm we only saw one. He could be in that room. We are definitely at the right house are we?"

"Of course we are. We've been here often enough."

"You've definitely spoken to Jacob before and seen him?"

"Yes. Look what are you getting at?"

"Well if he is as trapped as you say he is where is he? There is no sign of a male presence in the flat."

"He could be in the other bedroom."

"He could but from what you say she wouldn't want him there because he's a Jew so I would say it's unlikely."

"I don't know what to do," said Evelyn.

"There is nothing we can do," said an officer. "We can't break in because there is no proof of anything you have said being true."

"But it is. Why would we make it up?"

He shrugged. "I don't know. The best thing we can do is go back to headquarters and see what is happening about this so called SS officer you told us about."

They turned and went back the way they had come with looking back. The two women looked after them and then started moving themselves feeling very downcast.

"I can't believe this is happening," said Ingrid.

"Neither can I. I really thought this was the day we would be setting Jacob free."

"Me too."

"Well we better get moving in case arresting Sarah went pear shaped as well."

The two women walked briskly back hoping to find Bruno at his house. Ingrid knocked on the door and waited but got no answer.

Evelyn looked apprehensive as she turned to Ingrid saying, "It looks like he's been arrested and they are keeping him."

"Not necessarily. They may not have got round to speaking to him yet so don't despair before you have to."

Evelyn didn't look convinced. She got out her key and let themselves in. Once inside Evelyn went round calling Bruno's name but to be met with silence. "He's definitely not here."

"How about we go and see if we can find them?"

"We don't know where they meet, plus it could be risky if Sarah is still with him."

"I wasn't suggesting their meeting place, I was thinking of where they may have been taken for interviewing and imprisonment."

"I suppose we should."

"You don't sound so sure."

"I know it's just it seems wrong somehow as if we're thinking the worst case scenario. I can't bear the thought that he might be there either."

"I know but at least then we know what we're dealing with."

"True."

"Come on then. We have to face up to reality but at least we're together."

Evelyn set off at a jog. Now she'd got her mind on finding out she didn't want to waste anytime.

Ingrid puffing and blowing said, "Slow down…I can't…..keep up…"

"Sorry," said Evelyn very shamefaced. "You persuaded me that we needed to know so I got a bit carried away."

"That's ok, but we can go slower, it won't do any harm."

Evelyn slowed down to a walk but was still going at a quick pace. She just kept going not stopping for breath or anything. Ingrid found she was still having trouble keeping up.

It was a relief to the pair when they reached the building. By now familiar with the building they went straight up the steps and Ingrid spoke to the security guard with their query. They were directed to the same desk as the previous day. This time there was a queue so they stood in line waiting their turn. Evelyn rather impatiently it must be admitted.

"Calm down," whispered Ingrid. "There is nothing we can do except wait our turn."

"But it's taking so long."

"Not really. We've only been here a minute or two."

"It feels more like hours."

"Look there's Major Trott. Maybe he'll have news for us. I'll go up to him and leave you in the queue so we don't have to start again at the back."

Major Trott saw Ingrid walking towards him and approached her. "I thought you might have come here," he said grimly.

"Are you on your own?"

Ingrid shook her head. "Evelyn is waiting over there." She pointed to the queue.

"Go and get her then follow me."

Ingrid and Evelyn were almost running to keep up with the Major. They were taken to the same room as the day before. Once inside they took the seats the Major indicated.

"Right let's get down to business."

"This sounds ominous," said Ingrid.

"It is. You see Sarah denies all knowledge of being in the SS and living with anyone. She says she doesn't know anyone called Jacob. She admits to knowing Bruno and speaks openly about how sadistic he is. She used to be in a relationship with him and only keeps seeing him now because he won't let her go."

"What!" exclaimed the two women in unison. "It's the complete opposite. You believe her I suppose."

"It's not like that. But there is the issue that Jacob didn't seem to be anywhere to be seen at the house and there was no evidence that a male had even been there. My officers have checked with neighbours and they only know of Sarah. They commented on how nice and quiet she is. She keeps herself to herself so they haven't had a chance to get to know her."

"You have to believe us," said Ingrid in desperation.

"It's not that I don't, but at the moment it's your word against Sarah's."

"Sarah isn't even her real name. She only used that because it was Jacob's wife's name. If you knew her real name you might find her on your records."

"Do you think we're stupid. We've already done that and it led nowhere."

"What about Bruno?" asked Evelyn anxiously. She was realising they were just talking about Sarah and Jacob.

"We have to keep him in custody because of what he admitted yesterday which has been confirmed by Sarah today."

"What will happen to him?" asked Evelyn close to tears.

"It's not for me to say. The court will decide that. My best advice to you is that you forget about him and find yourself someone more suitable, instead of a known war criminal."

"But it's Bruno I love." She let the tears come, unable to hide them back anymore.

"Don't get upset. You'll realise in time it was for the best. You don't know when he might turn on you."

"He wouldn't. He's not like that," said Ingrid seeing Evelyn was beyond comment.

"But you don't know everything he's done."

"I know but he genuinely loves her."

"He might do but what happens if they argue as they will. All couples do. He could get violent. He obviously has a violent streak in him to do what he has."

The Major sounded so convincing that Ingrid even started to believe him even though she knew and had seem Bruno and Evelyn together. Besides it was difficult to argue as she couldn't deny he had done things that he shouldn't in the name of Hitler.

"What's happening to Sarah?" asked Ingrid.

"We've had to let her go."

"But what about Jacob. This will put him in more danger and Sarah won't have Bruno to meet so we won't be able to do anything about the situation."

"So you say but does this Jacob even exist?"

"We're not delusional you know. We are in our right mind, all three of us."

The Major raised his eyebrows in disbelief. He was finding it hard to be civil to these two women who seemed so certain their view was right and he was wrong. He was only going by evidence not emotions. Women, he thought, too emotional, letting their feelings rule their intellect.

He opened the door showing them that all discussion was over. He didn't even wish them a good day as they left. He breathed a sigh of relief hoping he wouldn't come across them again. Time wasters that's what they were. Just wanted a bit of attention.

He had been rather taken with Sarah who seemed so indignant and upset that anyone would say such things about her. She was just trying to get on with her life that was all. He thought how pretty she was and understood why Bruno kept tight hold of her, refusing to let her go. If he wasn't already married and a bit younger he would have been interested himself.

"Why don't you come back to mine?" suggested Ingrid. "You don't want to be on your own after that."

"Really I'd rather be alone. What if they release Bruno. He won't know where I am."

"We can leave a note for him," said Ingrid. "I just don't want to leave you at the moment and the chances of him getting out are very slim. The Major made it very clear."

"I know," sighed Evelyn. "I'm really worried about Jacob."

"Same here. Sarah really is a good actress isn't she. I really didn't think anyone would be taken in by her."

"Bruno has always said that. She can be very charming which is what he feel for in the first place. It was only later when he realised what she's really like."

Ingrid nodded. "We do need to go somewhere and discuss where we go from here."

"Mine then." There was silence until Evelyn added, "I've just had a thought. The house is in Bruno's name. Will I be able to stay here now he's gone."

"I'm not sure it would be safe for you to do so. Once word gets out about his past you could have an angry mob turning up on the doorstep."

"I hadn't thought of that. Maybe we're right and I should go to yours."

"You're very welcome to stay as long as you want or need to."

"Thanks. You're a good friend."

"I hope so."

They decided to go and pick up some of Evelyn's things so she wouldn't have to go back to the house anytime soon and then went on to Ingrid's flat.

Evelyn looked around. "It's nice and light which gives it more space."

"I know that's what I fell in love with when I came to view it. I knew straight away it was mine."

"Anyway I'll show you your room so you can drop your stuff off in there."

"Thanks," said Evelyn.

When Evelyn left the room she found Ingrid in the kitchen making a cup of tea for them and a sandwich.

"I don't think I could eat anything," said Evelyn.

"You have to eat. You won't help Bruno or Jacob if you don't have something. Just a little bit maybe."

"I'll be sick if I try."

Ingrid studied her pale face and the bruises under her eyes and thought how Evelyn had appeared to age in the last twenty four hours. She gave up trying to force her to eat seeing there might be some truth in what she had said.

They sat quietly sipping their tea, each lost in their own thoughts.

"What can we do?" asked Evelyn presently.

"I really don't know. We need to get to Jacob urgently. I'm still surprised the officers weren't that interested. They could have gained entry if they wanted to which would have revealed where Jacob was, but instead they just took in the situation at face value. It's as if they didn't believe us from the start."

"I know, although I hadn't thought of it like that."

"They are supposed to be neutral but it didn't seem to be like that."

"I know. They take one look at Sarah and that's it she's convinced them before anything is even said."

"If only a woman was investigating. A female wouldn't be so taken in by her."

"I understand what you're saying but don't see what we can do about it. Also it won't get them to break in to look for Jacob will it."

"I suppose not," said Ingrid.

They spent most of the evening quietly, talking about other subjects and avoiding the present one. They had decided that it could wait until the morning when it was fresh. It would be more likely that they would come up with some positive way forward which they mutually agreed.

Evelyn was quick to fall asleep having been more tired than she realised. She had been so sure she would be awake all night worrying but it didn't happen which Ingrid was pleased about when she looked in on her to make sure she was ok.

CHAPTER TWENTY

Sarah was furious by the time she'd got home. To be arrested and questioned like a common criminal. Of course, it was all Jacob's fault and he was going to hear all about it. If there weren't any Jews then she wouldn't have had to torture and kill them. She was doing the world a favour and to be treated like that. She shook her head as she opened the door.

Jacob, tied up in her bedroom, quavered when he heard the loud bang of the door. Something was obviously very wrong which meant she may take it out on him. He had heard the knocking on the door and window from his friends but he had no way of answering or calling out to them. Tape had been put over his mouth. It wasn't really a necessity but Sarah was revealing her true colours now.

"Grr. I'm so not happy," said Sarah entering her bedroom and kicking off her shoes. She picked one up and starting beating Jacob with it.

"If it wasn't for you Jews I wouldn't have been questioned about war crimes against humanity as they called it. We should have been allowed to get rid of you lot while we could. Doing the world a favour I was."

Jacob listened, still unable to respond.

"Go on have you got nothing to say?"

He stayed quiet he didn't even make a sound, thinking it better to say nothing and let her get it out. It wouldn't make any difference though she would still torture him. She was free to do what she liked and there was nothing he could do about it. While he was in her room tied and gagged he couldn't even tell his friends that things had got worse and had even become urgent.

"You know something, it's all your fault."

Jacob sighed inwardly. Surely she was repeating herself now. Did she have nothing original to say? What had made them arrest her, although he could guess. His friends had obviously told the authorities about what was happening but why then had she been released.

"It's a good job I'm such a good actress because the British Major believed me when I denied all knowledge. I even managed to gag as if I was going to be sick at the thought. Of course when they looked my name up they couldn't find me on their records because I gave them a false name. I'm not stupid."

Jacob became really frightened. How was he to get out of this now? She had lied and been believed, what would this mean for his future. He needed to get out and fast.

"I managed to convince them that my friend Bruno was the sadistic bitch that I am. They lapped it all up and now Bruno is locked up until his trial. I suppose I should be happy instead of furious."

Jacob thought she couldn't have liked Bruno as much as she made out if she was willing to give him up and lie about him so easily. Was she even capable of love for another human being? He wasn't convinced. His main thought now had to be getting out of there. He didn't know how because with Bruno locked up she would have no reason for disappearing for so long at a time and also while he was tied and gagged he couldn't do much. His only hope was that his friends would get taken seriously and they would come back with the British authorities again.

Sarah untied Jacob and took the tape off. He immediately stretched his arms and legs and stood up.

She disappeared for a minute or two before coming back with a cup of water and bread. "Here this is yours. You don't deserve anything else. I don't even know why I'm bothering to keep you alive. I could end it at any time."

Jacob said nothing, too focused on the bread and water.

"Got nothing to say. Ahh the poor Jew."

Jacob ignored her taunts, thinking it best to stay quiet. Hopefully she'd get tired of it and shut up. He had learned this tactic in the camps. Just shut up and let them do what they wanted, it was less likely to lead to punishment or death. It was just his luck to end up in this situation. Obviously when he was in hospital they hadn't picked up on her true character of they would have acted on it at the time. He would have had to put up with this.

Finishing the bread and water he passed them back to Sarah who took them to the kitchen.

"Ok I'm going to bed now. You can stand there as you did last night."

He couldn't stand it anymore and opened his mouth to say, "I need some sleep please can I lay down even if it's in the corner here."

"Sleep? Why should I allow you to sleep? You can stand there as if on role call and don't you dare slip down and try and sleep when you think I'm asleep. I'll know about it and you will be the worse off because of it."

Jacob said nothing, just stood there as requested. He was so tired and had no idea when she would let him sleep again. He found himself just wishing she would end it all as she talked about. Surely death had to be better than this. At least in the camp he had a few hours of sleep which was enough to keep him going. He had been young, fit and strong then, now he was neither.

His eyes started to close and he felt himself sliding down the wall. He opened his eyes and forced himself to stand again. This wasn't good, he was so tired that he was falling asleep standing.

Time went on. He wondered what time it was now and how much longer he would have to stand there. Sarah was fast asleep giving small snores occasionally. Surely she wouldn't noticed.

Again he felt his heavy eyes begin to close. He let them stay shut this time and slipped off into much needed sleep.

The next thing he knew, Sarah was shaking him, fury filling her face. "How dare you," she screamed at him. "I told you to stay awake and keep watch. You can't even do that can you, you stupid Jew."

What she didn't realise was that the walls were not thick and certainly at that loud pitch her voice could be heard by the neighbours.

"What was that?" asked a bleary eyed Stefan of his wife who was also sat up in bed.

"I don't know darling. It sounded like that lady next door. I can never remember her name."

"Sarah. I thought she lived on her own. At least she's the only one out and about. I thought she said once that her husband was killed at the end of the war trying to keep France in our hands."

"Then who is she screaming at? She seemed to call him a Jew."

"I know I heard. If it wasn't only two in the morning I'd go round and see if she's ok. You never can tell with all these foreign soldiers around to prey on lone, vulnerable women."

"She's never struck me like that though. She seems quite hard faced."

"True."

"Anyway all seems quiet now let's try and go back to sleep."

They settled down again and tried to sleep but found themselves tossing and turning both worried about Sarah.

……..

Bang! Bang! Came the knock on the door. Sarah groaned and got up to answer it.

"Yes?" she queried opening the door only slightly and peering round.

"We just wondered if everything was all right."

"Yes of course, everything's fine."

"That's good. Only we heard shouting in the night."

"Don't worry it was probably a bad dream." Sarah was definitely going to take this out of Jacob so he better watch out. It was all his fault that they had come to the attention of the neighbours.

The couple reassured for the moment went back to their own home.

"Jacob it's all your fault. Now I've got neighbours coming around to make sure everything is all right."

Jacob looked at her but said nothing. She got the gun from under the bed where it was being kept and pointed it at Jacob.

"If you shoot me they will hear even more and know something is wrong."

"I'll just tell them it was a British soldier broke in and attacked me. I'm sure I'll be convincing enough I always was a good actress. I can easily put on distress. I'll pretend the gun used is the soldier's."

Jacob wished he could do something, but didn't know what. She had taken the gag off but he was still tied up. If he screamed she'd shoot him for sure.

CHAPTER TWENTY ONE

Ingrid and Evelyn were sitting clutching their coffee cups and having the occasional sip of the scolding drink.

"What are we going to do?" asked Evelyn. "I feel as if it's down to us now. I hate to think what may have happened to Jacob after Sarah was released. I'm sure she took it out on him."

"That's what worries me," said Ingrid. "But I've been thinking. We should go round their and knock on the door asking for Jacob. She knows me so I'll keep out of sight. While you keep her talking I'll walk around and see if there is another door or window I could get in. Once inside I'll try and find Jacob and get him out."

"Do you really think that would work. I'm not so sure. It would take too long. I don't know what I can say that will keep her there."

"Have you got any better suggestions. As we have to do it on our own now. The authorities don't believe us and Bruno is locked up."

"We could just go and ask the neighbours. Or I can since we don't want you being seen by Sarah."

Ingrid was quiet for a minute thinking, then said, "Hmm. It might be worth a try I suppose. The neighbours might be more likely to open up to us than the authorities."

"Ok good plan. If you stay hidden at the end of the road I'll speak to the neighbours then come back and report to you what happened.

It was agreed. They had a leisurely morning, not wanting to go over too soon. Although Evelyn was not the most patient of people even she managed to wait, although there was a lot of pacing from one end of the room to the other which started annoying Ingrid.

"Can't you stop that?"

"No this is what I'm like when I'm waiting for something. I just can't settle, I have to do it straight away or else this happens."

"You really should learn patience."

"I think I'm too old to change now. If I was going to I would have when I was younger."

Ingrid nodded in agreement.

It seemed a very long day to both women and soon Ingrid was joining Evelyn with pacing and frequently checking their watches.

"See you're no better than me," said Evelyn.

"So it seems," responded Ingrid with a small smile.

"Come on, can't we go now?"

Ingrid checked her watch yet again and found it to be four in the afternoon. She nodded. It's probably as good a time as any. They got ready and left much to their relief. What a long day it had been.

On reaching the alley way leading to Sarah's house the two women parted company.

"Scream if you run into any problem," said Ingrid.

Evelyn nodded and went up the alley. On reaching the neighbours she knocked on the door.

"Hello," said Stefan opening the door slightly.

"Oh hello, sorry to bother you but I'm looking for Jacob who lives somewhere around here. I think next door."

"No, I've never met Jacob or any man next door. There's only a widowed lady called Sarah." Stefan paused before adding, "There was a bit of bother there in the night though. Woke me and my wife up it did with the screaming she was doing. Sounded like she was screaming at someone. I went round but she insisted everything was fine. Look why don't you come in for a minute."

"Thank you," said Evelyn as she stepped inside.

"Come through and take a seat. We don't stand on ceremony here."

Evelyn glanced around the room. It might look dingy and horrible outside but this couple had done the place up inside and had it looking like a tiny palace, strangely untouched by war and poverty.

"Nice," said Evelyn.

"We like it," commented Stefan. "Anyway what was it you wanted to know?"

"I was enquiring about a man named Jacob who lives next door with Sarah."

"That's new to us. She told us she was a widow on her own. But things didn't seem quite right last night when she started shouting at someone and mentioned Jew."

Evelyn paled. What had happened to Jacob?

"You all right love?" asked a concerned Lotte.

"Yes, it's just that Jacob is a Jew."

Lotte also paled at this news and looked across at her husband.

"It looks like she's been telling us some lies," said Stefan.

"What can we do to help?" asked a concerned Lotte.

"I'm not sure at the moment. Can I bring my friend along. She stayed at the end not wanting Sarah to see her as Sarah has met her before."

Evelyn rushed back to Ingrid and together they went back to speak to Stefan and Lotte. Ingrid was also concerned when she heard what the neighbours had to say.

"I think we need to get him out as soon as we possibly can," stated Ingrid.

The others nodded their heads.

"We really had no idea. It's terrible that we didn't know even though it was going on right under our noses. I know we didn't warm to Sarah but that doesn't mean anything. Some people like to keep to themselves for various reasons."

Stefan shook his head, struggling to come to terms with all that had been happening. He also felt guilty as if he should have known and stopped it sooner.

"Do you think if we go to the authorities it will make a difference. We are the neighbours after all and we heard the word Jew mentioned. They don't have to know you are involved at all."

Ingrid and Evelyn looked at each other and without consulting Evelyn, Ingrid agreed it was worth a try and might be the best option. Sarah was too volatile and had a gun so they wouldn't be able to do anything safely on their own. Even with four of them and the element of surprise it wouldn't work.

"We better get off. You are welcome to stay here so you can hear the news as soon as we get back. Hopefully we'll be accompanied by soldiers ready to search the place for Jacob."

"No we won't take up anymore of your space. You don't know us so we won't stay here. We'll wait for you in the park though."

"Great, that sounds good," said Stefan.

Lotte had been sitting there listening to what had been said but now she stepped in, "Why don't we all go. After all if they know you two so it might help to get your boyfriend free," said Lotte looking across at Evelyn.

Evelyn spoke, "That sounds a good idea, although if they'll take any notice if we are with you I don't know."

"Surely they'll have to. We are neighbours concerned with what we heard."

They all stood up and left the house. The nearer they got to the building the more nervous they became. Ingrid and Evelyn were unsure if they would be listened to and thought it might be better to wait outside. They didn't want it to all go wrong again. Ingrid suggested this but Stefan felt it would be better if they were all there together.

They went inside, Evelyn and Ingrid hanging back.

"Come on you two," said Lotte stopping and waiting for them.

They caught up and together the four approached the desk. It was Stefan who said why they were there.

Very soon they found themselves in an interview room facing Major Trott again.

"Not you two again," he sighed as he looked across at the two women.

Stefan spoke, "It was us. We persuaded them to come with us."

"And you are?"

"We're neighbours Stefan and Lotte."

"What have you got to say and make it quick, I have important things to be getting on with."

"This is important as well."

The Major sat there in silence listening to what Stefan had to say. His face grew grim as he listened. Ingrid glancing at him saw that he seemed to be taking this very seriously indeed.

"I really don't know how this could be happening. We were only there yesterday and there was no sign of a male presence"

"You didn't see into the other bedroom."

The Major shook his head. "It sounds as if we better investigate this further. I hope for your sake you are telling the truth as I will arrest you if not for wasting our time when we have real war criminals to deal with."

"It's all true as long as Sarah hasn't already done anything further."

"She wouldn't have had time surely."

"I think she would as if she is anything like most people she wouldn't have got back to sleep easily after shouting at Jacob."

The four left the building and went back. They were to stay at Stefan and Lotte's place waiting for it to be over or at least in their minds it would be over. If only it went according to plan.

They were all getting agitated and tetchy with each other by the time the soldiers arrived so they were glad of the distraction.

They watched out of the window and saw a couple of officers push their way passed Sarah and enter the house. This was hopeful and looked as if it would be all over soon.

....

Sarah was taken by surprise when the soldiers pushed their way into the house. She didn't understand what had gone wrong. Just the day before they had believed what she had to say now they were back.

"Sir," called one of them.

"Coming," called back the Major.

He rushed to where the others were. They moved aside to let him get through. The sight that met him brought him close to tears. Jacob was lying on the floor in the most awkward of positions with hands and feet tied up together. He was completely naked with raw wounds all over his back and buttocks. It looked as if he had been whipped within inches of his life. His eyes were closed. Major Trott knelt beside the body and checked for signs of life.

He looked up with a slight smile on his face, indicating Jacob was alive at least for the moment.

Sarah walked in and just for a moment her sadistic pleasure almost gave herself away but she recovered and looked devastating. "He's my brother. I don't know what happened to him. He won't talk about it."

"Why is he tied up in that position then?" asked Major Trott.

Sarah didn't answer. She couldn't think of an answer quick enough. Her silence said it all. She knew it was over, she had been well and truly caught.

"I suppose you are the SS guard you were accused of being as well."

Sarah stayed quiet. The less she said now the better.

"How could you. He's a vulnerable man. Don't you think he's been through enough already."

"He's still alive."

"Fortunately. I just hope he stays that way. Can one of you get an ambulance here quickly."

"Already done sir. They are on their way."

"Can you stay here. I need to go next door. Don't let Sarah move," said Major Trott giving her a quick glance of utter disdain.

Seating with the four next door he told them what they had uncovered and the state that Jacob was in.

"Can I go and see him?" asked Ingrid. "I'm a nurse."

"Yes please that would be really helpful."

It wasn't just Ingrid but the others all followed although it was only Ingrid who was allowed in the house. She gasped when she saw the state of Jacob. She had just heard it described but nothing could prepare her for the reality.

She confirmed he was alive but couldn't do a lot more. His wounds would heal in time but would leave permanent scars as a reminder of all he had been through. She looked at him lovingly and wondered if he would ever be able to trust anyone enough to share his life with them.

The four had the satisfaction of seeing Sarah being taken away assured by the Major that they would try and ensure she faced the maximum punishment, not just for war crimes but what she had done to Jacob as well.

"What about Bruno?" asked Evelyn tentatively.

"We will be interviewing him again. If things all add up I will personally request that he be let go. He seems to have changed and admitted he was wrong. Nothing would be served by sending him to prison."

EPILOGUE

One year later

"Stop fussing darling. It's all going to be ok," said Jacob to Ingrid.

"I know I just want to get it right."

"You will."

Ingrid and Jacob had been married for a month now and were having friends over for dinner for the first time as a married couple. This wasn't the first time the friends had been together but Ingrid still felt anxious as she was so new to this.

Ingrid and Jacob had been together ever since Jacob had been freed but they had taken things slowly. Jacob had needed time to grieve for his lost wife.

The bell rang and Jacob got up to get it. He gave a huge beam as he allowed Evelyn and Bruno to enter. He had a lot to thank the couple for. If it wasn't for them and Ingrid he would never have been in this position, happy, healthy and free. In fact he might not even be alive.

The four sat down to enjoy their meal. There was a lot of talking and laughter. Jacob looked around and felt comfortable with his friends and his lovely wife. He now had a future to look forward to. Ingrid, seeing his look, leaned towards him and took his hand giving it a squeeze. Evelyn and Bruno looked on with a huge smile. Everything had turned out well. They knew they would be friends for life.